Eleanor Talbot Kinkead

Florida Alexander

A Kentucky Girl

Eleanor Talbot Kinkead

Florida Alexander
A Kentucky Girl

ISBN/EAN: 9783337105211

Printed in Europe, USA, Canada, Australia, Japan

Cover: Foto ©Andreas Hilbeck / pixelio.de

More available books at **www.hansebooks.com**

Florida Alexander

A KENTUCKY GIRL

BY

ELEANOR TALBOT KINKEAD

AUTHOR OF " 'GAINST WIND AND TIDE," " YOUNG GREER
OF KENTUCKY," ETC.

CHICAGO
A. C. McCLURG AND COMPANY
1898

Florida Alexander

I

Upon the fragrant April morning a
voice rang out—the voice of a woman
singing in French a tender, pensive little
strain, but throwing into the song a
fervor, a profound sadness of interpretation such as the simple words and music
were never intended to evoke.

And such a voice! A warm contralto,
sonorous as the tones of a violoncello;
a voice to stir the blood and rouse into
instant quickening old memories that
have slept so long one almost fancies they
will never wake; a voice to tease, and
startle, and bewilder, until the brain
seems all a-whirl, and the world grows
dim and distant and lost in a mist of
tears. But though it had been artistic-

ally trained, it possessed only drawing-room capabilities, after all is said; and, in a way, St. John had often heard far better singers, even among amateurs, and forgotten their very names. Yet something in that passionate protest caught his ear, just as the ear is always caught at the first signs of genuine emotion. Is it because of a vague but ever-present consciousness of the universal heritage of sorrow that the heart so quickly responds to a cry of pain? He paused involuntarily beside the iron railing and looked intently toward the stately, white-pillared mansion beyond.

It was one of the houses he was accustomed to pass daily on the way to his collegiate duties. Being contemplative, he was inclined to make the most of his opportunities to observe the beautiful things of life, and he needed the opportunity only to perceive what a great many other people are apt to overlook. To go down that street, under the maples, implied nothing circuitous, but he would have been willing to take a considerable number of extra steps, on the days when he was not especially pressed for time, merely for the sake of the generous sense of latitude afforded by the sight of the picturesque old domicile, and for the pleasure of passing the wide, well-kept lawn, whereon the bluegrass flourished in such luxuriant growth. For this same bluegrass, as well as the denizens of the famous region of its perfection, had become a subject of interesting study to the young Bostonian during his eight months' sojourn in Kentucky; and he had found that there was no bluegrass, nor any person, more worthy of regard than the sward his eyes now rested upon and the gentleman to whom it belonged.

He appeared a reserved, polished young man of studious aspect and courteous but formal bearing. Of mere physical good, looks he possessed, perhaps, rather more than most; but the charm of his countenance was not revealed until he smiled or spoke. Then his face took on a certain brilliancy in the flash of white, even teeth against the swart but clear tone of his complexion. Slenderly and athletically built, he was tall, even among Kentuckians; and there was an agreeable contrast between his very black hair and deep blue eyes fringed with thick lashes. They were intensely earnest eyes, holding a rare purity in their depths. Perhaps there was about him a hint of austerity also. Above all, added to the marks of a more than ordinarily vigorous mentality, he bore the look of a man that holds always a firm grasp upon himself, the higher ideals of life being kept constantly in view.

It was the moral significance of this selfmastery, joined with a superior scholarship, that so strongly recommended him to the trustees of the State College at Lexington, who had offered him the chair of English Literature. Furthermore, it was thought that he would confer additional luster upon their institution, seeing that he had already attained considerable reputation as an author. And the professorship had been accepted; for Mr. Edward Winthrop St. John was one of that number who have found the writing of verse to be, at best, only a staff, and never at any time a crutch that may be relied on. However, he had discovered that life in this locality was not without interest, especially in the way of affording material for future literary work.

He had thoroughly familiarized himself with the romantic history of the State; had thrilled in reading the stories of the hardy pioneers, and longed for the Border Minstrel's pen that he might describe their fierce warfare while they wrested the land from the hostile bands that claimed it as their "happy hunting ground." Even further than to the Scottish annals, his imagination had been drawn backward to the old Homeric legends, to the heroes of ancient Greece; and in the Nibelungenlied, in Siegfried's adventures with bear and wolf and elk and buffalo, he found a counterpart of their perils with the savage beasts of the dark, untried forests.

With quickening pulse he had followed them, those brave men and braver women, as they fought their way through the wilderness, encountering every hardship and danger, but holding always to that dearest wish of the Anglo-Saxon heart, the founding of the home. Proving them loyal, intrepid, uncorrupted to the last, he had traced the course of this people through the long, heart-wearying struggle for statehood and the dazzling scheme of the Spanish Conspiracy, the rise of the political parties and the Old and the New Court controversy—on and on, he had followed them, down to the time of their action in the mournful tragedy of the Civil War, and in it all he had found much to honor and but little to condemn.

Socially, he had been well received, and no one had offered a more cordial hospitality than Major Ephraim Alexander, the owner of this delightful old Southern home. But the acquaintance did not include the sorrowful contralto, and for a moment it did not occur to St. John to identify her as a daughter of the house whose return, he knew, was expected, and of whom it would have been quite impossible not to hear a great deal.

As for that young woman, he had concluded that she must surely be the possessor of a most brilliant and potent personality to have impressed herself upon her townspeople in such flattering remembrance. For seldom had he touched upon the rather threadbare theme, the comeliness of Kentucky women, that some one did not instantly exclaim, "Ah, but you have never seen Miss Alexander—Florida Alexander; she is beautiful, really beautiful." And it had become with him a matter of interesting consideration that this unstinted praise so frequently proceeded from women who, justifiably, as it appeared, might have claimed the golden apple for themselves.

Furthermore, occasioned no doubt by the prospect of her return, both her outward and her inward loveliness had been such a frequent topic of conversation in a certain circle at that time, small wonder it was that the young professor, reasoning logically on the subject, found it difficult to reconcile those heart-broken tones with a being whom he had been forced to look upon as altogether blessed.

However, the question was decided at once. A peevish voice, raised high to drown the singing, cried impatiently in the hall, "Florida, Florida—for pity's sake!" There was a break in the music, and then the song came abruptly to an end.

A moment afterward, a young woman in a green serge gown and small round hat appeared in the doorway. She stood for an instant slowly drawing on her gloves, and looking up the street as if the glory of the bursting buds and blooms had broken newly upon her.

It was a long, narrow street, with deep,

grassy lawns and houses of varied archi-
tecture. Maples lined the sidewalk on
either side, and these reached forth their
arms to each other and formed a cool
archway of rustling green through which
the sunlight pierced in only occasional
rays like the fitful gleam of a spear.
There was an odor of locust in the air,
and here and there, toward the rear of
the buildings, the ground was strewn with
a pinkish, feathery fall, when the light
wind stirred the fruit-trees. The girl
seemed to yield herself to the earth's
beauty in a momentary abandonment;
then a preoccupied look crept into her
eyes. She came slowly down the long
stone pavement, fumbling nervously with
the buttons of her glove.

She was a tall young woman, svelte,
but well-rounded in figure, and she
walked with a swaying, graceful carriage,
a certain proud freedom of step that gave
an air of distinction. Beyond this, however, St. John thought that there was
nothing especially notable in her appear-

ance, in view of all that had been told him. He could see that her face was oval in contour, that she had light brown hair, and dark brown eyes, and a warm glow in her cheeks like the juice of a ripened pomegranate, her coloring being of the kind that generally attracts; but for his taste it was a trifle too pronounced.

Nevertheless, in spite of the utter unconventionality of the proceeding—and St. John was by no means one prone to disregard the conventionalities—he remained standing just where he had been arrested shortly before by that strange witchery in her voice. Some influence seemed to hold him now against his will.

But it was not until she had come quite near that he was able to give a name to the odd, unpleasant sensation that possessed him, and realized that it was disappointment—vague, shadowy, to be traced to a thin cloud of melancholy, perhaps, or regret—of something that life, thus far, had never given to him.

Her face was slightly averted, and it

was evident that she did not see him until her hand had touched the gate. Then, as in a swift bending she leaned above the latch, those bewildering, mournful brown eyes, of which already he had heard so much, were flashed deeply into his, and with a start, a pang of infinite sadness, he knew why it was that they called her beautiful, and saw that the pathos of her song was also written in her face.

With a certain grave dignity his hand involuntarily reached toward his hat, and turning, he walked quickly down the quiet, shaded street.

II

For the most part, the founders of the commonwealth of Kentucky were Presbyterians.

Of those vigorous Scotch-Irish settlers who, more than a century ago, removed from the Valley of Virginia to the Kentucky solitudes, none were more honorable than the Alexanders. Shortly after the Revolution, one of the name had penetrated to this land beyond the mountains, bringing back such accounts of its primeval beauty, the denseness of the magnificent forests, the richness of the soil, and the luxuriance of the vegetation, that, ere long, many of his kinsmen were eager to follow him into this new Paradise, where their desire for landed possession—relic of an older civilization— might be gratified to the full. Having

established themselves here, they inter-
married with other prominent Virginia
families, who likewise had been induced
to make their homes in this favored region.

The move proved an advantageous one
to the Alexanders, for the free life of the
wilderness was conducive to health, and
their prosperity steadily increased. But,
through all the years, their position
seemed to rest less upon a certain stateliness, which in time appeared in their
surroundings, than upon the solid dignity
of a profound religious conviction, the
character growing out of an unswerving
allegiance to the faith; so that to-day
one could find an excellent example of
the courtly graces of the Cavalier com-
bined with the stern principles of the
Scotch-Irish Presbyterian in Major
Ephraim Alexander, the oldest, as well
as the ablest, representative of this ancient
stock.

At sixty-nine he was a remarkably
youthful-looking man. His abundant

dark hair, streaked with silver, fell about a brow of singular vigor, and his commanding form was still borne soldierly erect. Something of the fire of other days seemed to lurk in his piercing black eyes; but if one intuitively dreaded the power of his glance when directed against injustice and the evil-worker, this suggestion of severity was belied by an expression of rare sweetness and benevolence about the sensitive mouth.

A graduate of old Transylvania University, and accustomed from his youth to a familiarity with the best literary thought, his early taste for the classics never left him; and such was his acquaintance with the Greek and the Latin tongues that woe it was to that aspiring young Kentucky orator, fresh from one of the colleges, who dared misquote in his presence—presuming upon a supposed inaccuracy of knowledge regarding the defunct languages on the part of his auditors.

Conservative in his judgments, politically he was a patriot of the order that knows no bias for selfish interests. He had taken an active part in the stirring issues of the Civil War period; and it is to the deliberation, the wise counsel of such men as he, prior and subsequent to the great contest, rather than to their actual service, that the impartial future historian of Kentucky must give the greater honor.

But that dark period of internecine strife had long been past. And if certain portions of his existence had been tumultuous and wind-swept, he appeared now to have entered the harbor of a serene and beautiful old age delightful to witness.

It seemed to Florida that he was strangely unaltered in appearance by the three years. So painful and eventful had been most of that time to her, it was difficult to realize the smooth tranquillity of his even days. How she had longed to see him! yet always with that touching solicitude that shrinks so pitifully from

the marks of feebleness and decay upon
one beloved. But when, with his old-
time courtesy, he rose to greet her on the
evening of her return, something—something in the gentle tones of his voice,
perhaps—brought back a piercing re-
minder. The old wound in her heart,
which time seemed wholly inadequate to
heal, was opened anew. Suddenly the
light of her childhood had gathered about
her; a mist had sprung into her eyes.

And again they were living quite alone
together in the old house—just her father
and herself—in such companionship as
she knew could never more return. She
could see herself as she appeared in those
days—a slender, earnest little creature,
with wide, wistful brown eyes, and long,
unruly hair falling about her face—now
flitting restlessly from room to room,
now sitting demure and important opposite her father at table, or climbing up on
the rounds of his chair to receive the
good-night kiss. And those had been
such pleasant days, hallowed as they were

by shadowy recollections of the beautiful mother who had faded so strangely out of her life, and of the little dead brothers and sisters whose voices she often seemed to hear calling to her at her play, or when alone in the quiet nursery. Then that crushing, agonizing moment when it first broke upon her childish consciousness that everything was to be changed! There was to be a new mother, whom she was told that she must love. On the night after this announcement they searched for her long and in vain. And when in the murky morning light she returned, the dank cemetery leaves clinging to her garments, there was that written in her countenance which never left it in all the years to come. She remembered that they had said then: "She is so young—a mere child; she will surely get over it." But she alone knew that she never would get over it.

And so it had come about that her home-coming was always more or less painful, and this last home-coming was especially painful because of many things. She had lived on a kind of breathless tension for much of the past three years; and she had deeply suffered— as every one must suffer whose existence has been in any degree a yielding to an impulse of nature in indifference to the law of conscience. Life had seemed all at once to break upon her with such overwhelming force. The current had been so swift and strong, at first she had been exhilarated; then bewildered and baffled and terrified with dread.

On the morning after her return, Florida sat long in one of the deep chairs in her pretty bedchamber. In some of the rooms her stepmother had seen fit to make certain alterations; but this little nook had been left unchanged. Everything was startlingly familiar; the same small white bed with its muslin hangings, the same pictures in their old places, the same airy furniture, and cool chintz, and wild roses on the walls. Once it had been her mother's room; and though

Florida Alexander

Florida could recall only a few incidents to mark the association, in some dim, devotional way she had always felt that here a kindly spirit hovered near—the spirit of the long-dead mother of whom the girl thought so often and so tenderly, and of whom in reality she knew so little. But it had been told her that her mother—the home of whose people had been in the far South, the family having removed to Kentucky at a much later period than the Alexanders—was of French descent. Florida herself seldom spoke the name. There was an exquisite ivory miniature, set in pearls. She rose and took it from its case, and looked for some time upon the lovely features. It was a willful little face, gay and debonair, yet womanly and sweet withal.

As she returned it to its enclosure and placed it for safe-keeping in a secret drawer in her desk, her eye was caught by a book hid carefully away in the farthest corner. She reached forth a hand to it, and as her glance fell upon the cover an amused expression crept into her eyes. Her journal! What girlish rhapsodies and high-flown moralizations would she find here? With a flickering smile playing about her lips, she carelessly turned the leaves. The last entry had been made nearly five years before. In a clear, strong hand she had written:

"A dull day. Leaden skies overhead, a sense of depression within. Why—why am I always so sad? But I scarcely know what I want. I wonder if the desires of other people are any more definite. Or is this restlessness common to all humanity? If only I could shake off the feeling of restraint, of incompleteness, the consciousness that only one half of me is living, while the other half is being slowly starved.

"But, oh! the great sorrowful, suffering world! And how despicable to think only of one's own happiness—or the want of it, which is putting it far more correctly in my case.

"On Wednesday one of my friends is

to be married—actually one of my friends. I passed her house this afternoon; she was standing at the window, and she beckoned to me to come in. She showed me her wedding-gown, a most royal affair of gleaming satin and rare old lace. I could not speak; yet Marie chatted volubly, and was all the time quite cool and unconcerned.

"I wonder if I shall ever be married? I think I should rather not. But how strange to go to one's grave and never to have known what to some has meant so much."

And beneath this she had scribbled in pencil, as if half in derision, some lines from "Maud," which were evidently an afterthought:

> "Let the sweet heavens endure,
>   Not close and darken above me
> Before I am quite, quite sure
>   That there is one to love me;
> Then let come what come may
>   To a life that has been so sad,
> I shall have had my day."

Florida Alexander

The book fell from her grasp; she had grown very pale. The folds of her delicate pink morning gown trembled as they fell about her; she was quivering in every nerve. Her dark eyes grew thrillingly intense, tragically beautiful. She stood a moment, wrapped in deepest meditation, her hands clasped behind her head. Then, as if shaking off by a mighty effort the thoughts that had come surging in upon her, she turned, walked quickly from the room and down the long stair, and paused beside the library door. A low, musical voice responded to her knock.

She found her father alone among his books.

III

Florida stood a moment, irresolute, on the threshold.

The Major was seated in a carved, high-backed chair near the fire, his Homer open before him and a volume of Sir Walter on the table close at hand. There was a look of keen enjoyment upon his fine patrician features, as in martial pomp the old Grecian and Trojan warriors stalked before his fancy. His rare physical beauty seemed heightened by the effect of the room's quaint picturesqueness.

It was a charming room to read in, or to dream in, as one might feel inclined; and it was especially inviting this moist April morning, for a light rain was beginning to fall, and the cheerful wood fire on the hearth gave a sense of warmth and comfort not elsewhere to be found. The polished andirons winked in the ruddy glow. An aged setter dozed upon the rug. The firelight gleamed upon massive book-cases filled with the works of delightful authors, and upon old silver candelabra and rich brocade hangings. Scattered through the room were many interesting relics suggestive of earlier days; and on the wall there were a number of dim family portraits—portraits, most of them, of distinguished officers in the Revolutionary and the Colonial wars—whose eyes seemed to follow the occupant with such stern, persistent accusation that one felt half-disposed to fall on his knees before them and make a clean breast of all his sins and shortcomings, vowing there and then to renounce these one and all forever, if only their countenances would in some small degree relax. It is not recorded that they ever did relax, perhaps for the reason that no one ever actually made the confession. It may be doubted that one ever, even though willing, tells everything. However, something at least approaching a confession rose, like an offering of incense, before them on this particular morning. Florida was in a strange mood.

"Do I disturb you, papa?" she asked timidly, drawing back, her whole attitude, nevertheless, expressing an appeal.

Her father looked up quickly from his book, and the warmth of an especial welcome overspread his face.

"Is it you, my dear? Come right in—come right in!" he cried heartily. "No, *no*," seeing that she still hesitated, "you do not disturb me." He carefully placed a mark in the place where he had been reading, and pushing back his spectacles rose with old-time courtliness.

Florida sat down in a low chair at his side. Her head sank back a little languidly against the silken cushion. The firelight deepened the color of her gown to a rosier tint. "How nice and warm you are here, papa. And the dear old room!" she exclaimed softly.

Her eyes swept the apartment with a

slow, caressing gaze. Presently she leaned toward the book he had just laid aside. "May I see where you were?" she asked, brightening at the sight of the familiar Greek text. Her glance ran swiftly over the page, her face expressing something of the same eager interest one feels in confronting the features of a friend after a long separation. "Ah, the parting of Hector and Andromache. How beautiful it is—always beautiful!"

The Major's face glowed with a kindred enthusiasm. "Do you recall Pope's lines in the translation, my dear? Let me see—how do they run?

'Andromache, my soul's far better part,
  Why with untimely sorrows heaves thy heart?
  No hostile hand can antedate my doom
  Till fate condemns me to the silent tomb.'"

And in his gentle, beautifully modulated voice he recited the stanza, just as Florida had heard him recite it, preceded by precisely the same inquiry and with the same perfect intonation, from the days of her earliest recollection.

"What a fatalist of the fatalists he was, papa—Hector, son of Priam! But his must have been rather a comfortable doctrine, on the whole, if calculated to make one a trifle incautious.

' No hostile hand can antedate my doom
Till fate condemns me to the silent tomb.'"

She repeated the lines thoughtfully, as if weighing their secret meaning.

The light of a secure and holy faith shone in her father's face; again he was ready with a quotation:

" 'Dimly of old in such scenes and sufferings men saw fate; now they see God,' " he responded fervently.

Florida's eyes wandered away to the curling lilac flames on the hearth. She leaned forward on her elbow, growing grave and pensive.

"It would be beautiful to be able still to see God, even in all the sufferings of the world," she said, at length, dispiritedly, "if we only could, if we only could." A huskiness had crept into her voice, and her erect figure seemed suddenly bowed. "But it has always appeared to me that most of the suffering we have to bear only comes through our own wrong-doing; we are simply reaping the whirlwind," she added quickly.

A tremor swept her frame. She threw an uneasy glance over her shoulder, as if shrinking from some haunting presence. She was silent. She sat nervously twisting her long, white, ringless fingers in an absent fashion. When she next spoke her manner was slightly abrupt and constrained.

"I came to tell you a little of myself this morning, papa—something of the past three years. Letters give so little. I so much feel the need of guidance."

Her father's face wore an expression of amiable attention, as if he were about to listen to the prattle of a child.

"There isn't very much—to speak of," she supplemented with a slight emphasis, which, however, his ear did not detect. "In the first place, I think an explanation of everything as regards myself may be found in the continual warring of certain inherent elements of my own nature—in other words, in the principle of heredity.''

The Major's somewhat reluctant entrance into the shadowy depths of these most uncertain waters passed unnoticed, and she hurried on.

''To a temperament particularly fervid and self-indulgent, there was added an altruistic sense—a sense of awful human responsibility.'' As clearly and as indifferently as one might reveal the characteristics of another she presented her analysis. ''Then at college I came under certain influences, especially the influence of a sister of one of my friends. This girl—woman, rather (she was years older than any of us)—was often at our rooms. She was a remarkable person, one of the plainest and, at the same time, most beautiful people I ever saw. Her whole soul seemed absorbed in the college settlement idea, the work of the city missionary, and in other great charitable plans that have for their object the relief and enlightenment of the poorer classes. Through my acquaintance with her the longing I have always had to be one of the practical workers of the world increased. There are so many sorrowful, needy ones, my heart so often ached at the thought of them. And at times I felt irresistibly drawn to go forth and give my efforts, whatever money I should have, my entire life, to the cause of mercy. But these moods of exaltation, of self-surrender, were always followed by the dullness of reaction." She broke off suddenly with a hopeless gesture of utter weariness. "If I truly wanted to live for others," she continued sadly, after a moment, "I just as truly wanted something of life for myself. I was strong, I was young—still on the very threshold of existence—I could not help feeling that somewhere—somewhere in the great sad world individual happiness was yet to be found; and I was not quite able to put all chance of reaching it for-

ever out of my grasp. Finally there
came a moment when a decision must be
made. Aunt Augusta's invitation to
come to her in Baltimore after my gradu-
ation and Ethel Strong's letter from New
York asking me to unite with her in her
work came to me by the same mail. For
weeks I could not sleep. At length I
made my choice; and I chose in favor of
self, of the world." Her voice died away
in a sob.

"You were far too young for the work,
whatever it was, my dear," the Major in-
terposed, somewhat mystified and not a
little impatient. "It was altogether
proper that you should go to your aunt."

The girl lifted her eyes filled with an
inexpressible pathos to his.

"Papa, can you not see that it was a
choice for eternity?" she cried bitterly.
"The highest was presented to me, and I
—I could not take it. It will never be
offered again. But I suffered so—I *suffered* so in trying to find happiness."

There could be no denial of the ring of

despairing pain in the low, vibrant voice, quivering with emotion.

In the surprise of a sudden revelation her words broke upon her father's ears, startling him to a recognition of something which now for the first time had begun to dawn upon him: the fact of her broadened womanhood, her intense capacity to feel. A sense of inadequacy took possession of him, and he was conscious of a most distressing uncertainty as to the best method to be employed in dealing with her. In helpless confusion his mind ran back to the women of her race, especially to those nearest him, of his own blood. They had all been gentlewomen in a high meaning of the word. But these had been content to find their duties in the home, dispensing whatever charities they felt inclined to at no farther distance from the domestic circle than the rear of their own habitations, thus manifesting a modesty which to him appeared not only becoming but entirely indispensable. This latter-day young woman, with her restless eagerness to take upon herself the solution of problems with which older and far wiser heads have been unable successfully to cope, very ill accorded with his unalterable standards. He was disturbed as well as mortified that, even in what he considered the mere freak of a moment, a child of his should have adopted any of the advanced ideas regarding the position of women, views which to him were most improper and distasteful, especially in one so young.

"What did your Aunt Augusta have to say to you on these subjects?" he asked anxiously, studying the girl's face above his gold-rimmed spectacles.

"I never discussed them with Aunt Augusta. After I went to her, I was involved in a perpetual whirl of gayety and travel, and all the shams and mockeries of the society she leads in. Besides, I had made my choice; I was no longer worthy of a place among those earnest, true-hearted women who were laboring to

lighten the burdens of others, and I felt
I ought not even to take their names
upon my lips.''

''Fanciful, wholly fanciful, my dear.''

She drew a little nearer to him, half-
crouching at his side.

''I have been playing with coals of fire,
papa,—what wonder is it that I got
burned?'' She quickly put up both of
her hands to her eyes, as if to still their
dull ache. ''But oh, there is always so
much needless pain—and the blunders,
the hopeless, irretrievable blunders!''
Then in a perfect passion of self-pity, she
broke forth, as she lifted her head: ''I
was so young—I had no mother!''

Involuntarily and unconsciously the
words from Browning's great tragedy had
come to her lips—words of which Dickens
once wrote, ''I know nothing that is so
affecting, nothing in any book I have
ever read.''

There were hot tears on her cheeks;
she turned away her face.

The Major rose, and began to move

slowly up and down the room, his hands clasped behind him, his brows knit in disquieting thoughts.

But when he finally resumed his seat his countenance had cleared. A remedy was beginning to unfold itself. Undoubtedly, in his opinion, the cause of the girl's morbid and untranquil state of mind was to be traced to the effect of the light, unsound literature flooding the country on every hand. Much that the critics of the day held in high estimate he regarded as sensational if not positively pernicious in its tendency. He was grieved to discover that he had allowed her to be away from his influence long enough, possibly, for her youthful tastes to be somewhat contaminated. But, fortunately, it was not too late to mend this error. He laid his hand with a mild firmness upon her shoulder.

"From now on you must begin and read good books," he said, his customary benign repose having wholly returned. "Imbue your thoughts with the lofty conceptions of those grand old authors that immortalized themselves in the past. Most of this modern writing is mere worthless stuff, unfit for you to read. The right plan is to begin the day with an hour or two devoted to Scriptural reading. As Dr. Watts expressed it—

> 'The testimonies of thy grace
> I set before mine eyes,
> There I derive my daily strength,
> And there my comfort lies.'

"You might review your Greek and Latin," he continued, "reciting to me, including also a series of metaphysical studies which I will map out for you. Then, for lighter reading, take up Macaulay's essays, and Addison, allowing yourself occasional glimpses, at my direction, into the 'Noctes Ambrosianæ.' These, with Shakespeare, Milton, Southey, Pope, Coleridge, Goldsmith, Burns and Wordsworth, together with the novels of Sir Walter Scott and Miss Edgeworth, will bring about a total change of ideas, developing in you, furthermore, certain delightful conversational powers which you should strive to cultivate, and which the young women of the present generation appear to me sadly to lack.''

At this rather alarming distribution of her time and labors, Florida experienced one of those ·swift changes of mood the capacity for which constituted her subtlest charm. A gleam of merriment shot from under her downcast lids.

''I have read them all, papa, again and again—the very last one of them; but, at your suggestion, I will begin with them again, and see what they can do in the way of restoring a perverted mind to a more healthful condition.''

She sprang lightly to her feet, a half-serious, half-comic expression flitting across her features. She stood a moment resting her arms, with their ruffles of filmy lace, upon the carved back of his antique chair. ''Do you remember your old term to describe me?'' she asked, bending caressingly above him. '' 'Fantastic' it was, wasn't it, papa? I used to think it rather applicable. I could even see the appropriateness myself. And the 'hair-brained, sentimental trace,' do you still find that, too, papa? I had thought I must have lost it in the weariness of the years.''

Her father's indulgent ·smile was a relief, after the high tension.

''You have not lost it yet,'' answered the Major, slowly shaking his head. ''Be assured, you have not lost it yet.''

IV

Among the Arabs there is an old prov-
erb which tersely mentions three things
that never come back: the word that has
been spoken, the arrow that has been sent,
and the opportunity that has been lost.
Shortly after he came to Kentucky, St.
John experienced a melancholy realization of the truth of the last clause of this
apothegm on the occasion when he first
met Mrs. Alexander.

From what he had heard concerning
her, he half-expected, as he was ushered
into her presence, to find her reclining in
white on a silken divan, arrayed in a blue
gauze scarf, and reading aloud from one
of her manuscripts to an admiring coterie,
after the fashion of Delphine Gay. As
a matter of fact, however, he discovered
little in the appearance of the majestic,

dark-haired matron of fifty, whose glances coldly swept his face, suggestive of the portraitures that have come down to us of the ethereal goddess of the salôn, who was wont to assume unto herself the imperious designation of "Muse of the Nation." For whatever marks of mental similarity might possibly exist, it was evident that physically Mrs. Alexander's distinction rested upon claims of a far more munificent if less airy description. Although there still remained traces of that rare perfection of feature which, a quarter of a century before, had caused her to stand out preëminent in a renowned galaxy of Louisville beauties, at most these traces were now only the vaguest hints that threatened soon to be entirely lost in a robustness fatal to classic proportion. In the meanwhile, she was, nevertheless, a notably handsome woman; and St. John saw at once that she was something more than a handsome woman—in short, a personage by no means to be overlooked. Furthermore, he recognized that it was due entirely to his own denseness in this memorable experience that he failed to grasp the fortune of her favor.

The occasion was that of one of her brilliant evening receptions, and the goddess, gorgeously attired, and rather dazzling in her splendor, had swept down upon him with especial effect.

With a magisterial assumption that was wholly sincere, during the course of the next fifteen minutes she plunged with such bold assault into literary topics that, in spite of the compliment implied, St. John, who was apt to be a little constrained on meeting with strangers, was completely routed and silenced. Beginning with the early Victorian poets, she proceeded rapidly, finally drifting into a tedious dissertation on the subject of the Pre-Raphaelites, and concluding, either through want of breath or further knowledge in this direction, with a brief survey of William Morris and an enigmatical reference to the ''Earthly Paradise.''

Florida Alexander

St. John's worst enemy, if he had
one, would have been unable, with any
show of truthfulness, to attribute to him
the fault of holding himself in too high
estimate; but in the course of this remarkable monologue, he was conscious of
an uncomfortable sensation of growing
steadily less, and that with such alarming
rapidity it was to be doubted that he
could ever, except with the aid of a
microscope, succeed in finding himself
again.

That he was, indeed, far from acquit-
ting him with the brilliancy that would
have redounded to his credit was coldly
manifest in the expression of his recon-
dite hostess. After a pause, in which
abundant time was given him to soar to
the heights she had just been scaling, she
turned disgustedly away, never again
deigning to bestow her erudition upon
him. However, in spite of this lament-
able failure on his part, she continued to
honor him with her invitations, and the
young man was thus given an opportun-

ity, though from afar, for the study of a type which he found peculiarly suggestive.

He noted that she posed a good deal, and that she had rather a sagacious eye for effects. One picture stood out with a kind of ironic boldness; and he seldom thought of her that she did not in the same instant appear before his mental vision royally seated in her salôn, wearing a yellow satin gown, and with her two little girls in white muslin, their piquant, gypsy faces eager with interest in the conversation of their elders, gracefully grouped about her knees.

Perhaps the hint of maternal devotion, admirably displayed, was somewhat denied by the lateness of the hour and the unfitness of the topic under discussion for childish ears; but the impression was one that he long retained. . Moreover, he found that in another line also she was capable of making for herself a good name with apparently as little effort.

Precisely upon what Mrs. Alexander's reputation as a great authoress was based,

St. John found some difficulty in ascertaining. No one, as far as he could discover, when actually brought to the issue, seemed able to point to a single publication from her pen; but that she did enjoy this reputation, somewhat presuming upon it, there could not be the smallest doubt. And the fact that there was a certain mystery attached to her literary proceedings appeared only to enhance their importance. It was whispered that for years she had been engaged upon the composition of a work that would surely render her famous, if not immortal; but the nature of the work and the time of its probable appearance were veiled in an obscurity that no one had ever penetrated.

When St. John wearied of this study in a circle, as he sometimes did, there were other persons scarcely less interesting whom he was accustomed to meet at this hospitable mansion; beautiful young girls whose soft Southern speech and simple high-breeding delighted him, and cordial, manly young men whom he found it easy to like, but not always easy to apprehend. Above all, there was always the Major.

Between this scholarly gentleman of a bygone day, with his lofty scorn of all recent literary methods, and one of the most modern of modern young authors, there had sprung up a rare sympathy and warmth of admiration. Accordingly, on Mrs. Alexander's Monday evenings, some of St. John's pleasantest moments were spent before the Major's library fire, away from the babel of tongues in the drawing-room, while he listened to the mellow tones of a voice that thrilled him like a strain of old-time music. But the drawing-room was now to have a new attraction — the attraction of the Major's daughter.

She had been at home for about a week when St. John received one of Mrs. Alexander's characteristic missives, which always reminded him of a royal mandate. He found the note lying on his desk one afternoon, on returning rather later than ordinary from his duties at the college. He smiled grimly as he broke the seal. Five hours in the class-room was scarcely a preparation for that agreeable frame of mind with which he could have wished to approach the sacred token of her bidding; for Mrs. Alexander was evidently of the opinion that genius always expresses itself in hieroglyphics.

As he applied himself to the difficult task of deciphering her message, he much regretted that she had not seen fit to imitate the example of the considerate Frenchman who, in addressing his archbishop, thus modestly expressed himself: "Out of respect for you, sir, I have written this with my own hand, but to facilitate the reading I send a copy which I have had my amanuensis make." He very much doubted that Mrs. Alexander possessed either a similar modesty or— an amanuensis!

However, he finally made it clear to himself that his presence was desired for the following Monday evening, and that the occasion was to differ somewhat from her usual informal gatherings, being musical rather than strictly literary, a departure which her mystic pen had dubbed ''a hazard of dubious diversion.''

St. John was beginning to reach the age when most men adjust themselves more or less to the inevitable law of compromise. But thus far he had never been able to bring himself to anything approaching a compromise in the way of music.

He had just fashioned in his mind some gracious form of excuse in which he congratulated himself as appearing sufficiently appreciative not to call down an unrelenting ire, when suddenly he bethought himself of Miss Alexander's voice. He sat a moment, pen in hand, recalling the pathos of those wondrous tones.

Then, with the exactness which he always employed, even in small matters, he carefully wrote an acceptance, sending the note at once.

V

St. John's modest habitation—a one-
story frame cottage of three or four
rooms—had been selected on account of
its pleasant location on a shady street,
remote from the din and traffic of the
town.

Outwardly, it was far from what the
young man's artistic taste would have preferred, being painted a vivid green, supplemented with yellow trimmings of a
most aggressive order. However, there
was a refreshing little grass-plot in front,
a spreading elm, as well as two picturesque apple-trees, now in full bloom and
breathing the very essence of promise,
the dawn and delicacy of the spring-tide.
His poet-nature, especially sensitive to
all environment, seemed absolutely to
demand some contact, limited though it

might be, with the growing things of earth; and his earnest reserve rendered an existence in the average boarding-house or hotel wholly insupportable. But his incipient attempts at housekeeping, characterized by a man's broad but clumsy methods, had been fraught with difficulties unsuspected in his calculations.

In the first place, little did he anticipate that an obscure advertisement in one of the daily newspapers expressing a desire on his part for a competent servant to take charge of his ménage, and briefly stating his terms and requirements, etc., would bring down upon him such a plague in the way of colored applicants as was equaled only by the swarm of flies that descended upon Pharaoh and the Egyptians of old. At all events, for weeks after this notice appeared, in season and out of season, through fair and through stormy weather, he was besieged with a persistence that would have been truly exasperating had there not been a touch of drollery in the experience of an entirely novel order. And it was not until some time after he was comfortably established, and the unfamiliar dialect had ceased to sound continually in his ears that he discovered the blunder he had made.

Out of the multitudinous throng presenting a strange dissimilarity as to costume, age, and characteristics, his bewildered faculties had been able finally to select one who he thought would prove best suited to his needs—an able-bodied, elderly person of neat appearance, whose twinkling eyes, set in an ebon countenance, seemed to express an intelligent amiability.

In answer to his puzzled inquiry one day concerning his first mistake, the woman stood for a moment with both hands on her broad hips, smilingly regarding him with an air of astuteness as well as of affectionate condescension.

"Honey," said she, at length, as if volunteering an explanation to a child, "I *tell* you. You ought never tuh said nothin' 'bout what you gwine pay. Wait an' ax 'em fust what they been gittin'. That old nigger Abram," breaking into a generous grin at the reminiscence, "that old nigger Abram he seed it in th' paper, an' th' preacher done give it out in meetin', an' all them darkies commenced a-chucklin' tuh theyse'f, thinkin' how easy 't would be tuh cheat yo' ve'y eyes out, while you gone long tendin' tuh yo' bus'ness, an' they hur eatin' they haids off, hangin' over th' front gate, an' gittin' bigger wages thin anybody else."

"Am I really giving better wages than anybody else, Aunt Phyllis?" asked the young man, amused, having readily adopted the usual local method of address when speaking to her.

The woman dropped her eyes.

For a moment she appeared a trifle disconcerted, but she was equal to the occasion. With a superb gesture, she raised her powerful form to its full height.

"Ef you *is*," she asserted, with stern impressiveness, "all *I* got tuh say, ef you *is* givin' better wages, *you gittin' better work!*"

And with the triumphant logic of this rejoinder, it was evident that she considered the matter finally dismissed; for she maintained a proud reticence concerning it in the future that no teasing innuendo was able to disturb.

Perhaps it was there and then that she fully assumed an authority in his affairs which St. John never afterward dared dispute. In point of fact, she proved herself invaluable in many ways, especially as a toothsome cook of the good old Southern style; and if occasionally he had reason to suspect her of the fault she was so ready to attribute to others of her race, he displayed a wisdom that older housekeepers might do well to imitate: he simply refused to see that anything went amiss. Under this discreet system of management they proceeded most amicably, and as time went by, her watchful care and attention and her good-natured chidings as well, were among the pleasantest things in a life peculiarly isolated and barren of affection.

He spent most of his evenings in his cheerful little sitting-room among his books. He had succeeded in making the place seem quite attractive in a very simple way, with the aid of shaded lamps and rugs and comfortable chairs. There were several good etchings on the walls, and a wide table covered with magazines and papers and materials for writing, which gave a certain tone. But something, a mere touch somewhere, perhaps, was wanting, and St. John felt it, and lamented it, though scarcely referring his regret to the proper source.

On the evening of Mrs. Alexander's musical he had been re-reading *Marius the Epicurean*, especially the story of Cupid and Psyche, the most beautiful, because the most human, of all the old mythological legends, and rendered even more beautifully human by the pure diction of Walter Pater. One expression, above all others, remained, like a golden thread inlaid in ivory and intricately traced, "the hiddenness of perfect things."

After he had laid the book aside, he leaned far back in his chair, closed his eyes, and gave himself, as was his wont, wholly up to the train of thought into which his imagination drove him. One of the windows was open, and the warm night air, heavy with perfume, stole languidly into the room, teasing his senses with a dim suggestion of some far-off, perfect realm—an existence, alluring, delightful, yet never to be attained—*the ideal life!* Unconsciously the moments slipped.

He was hours past the appointed time when he finally presented himself in Mrs. Alexander's crowded drawing-room.

The affair was on a more extensive scale than he had anticipated.

He had just reassured himself that for this reason his tardiness could scarcely have been considered, when his hostess, regal in a ruby-colored velvet gown, and blazing with jewels, bore severely down upon him.

"I fear I must ask your gracious indulgence," he began, as he came forward. There was always a formality, a unique picturesqueness in his flawless courtesy. And it was most characteristic of the simple sincerity of his nature that he added quickly, in slight embarrassment:

"I had been reading, and the time passed."

Mrs. Alexander regarded him abstractedly for a moment with eyes that seemed to see and yet not to see him.

"You *are* late," she assented, at length, with thinly veiled displeasure. "However, I believe there is still another number on the programme." She spoke in cold, metallic tones, suggestive of some inward irritation.

At this moment a group at the far end of the long room parted, and a young woman advanced toward the piano. Florida! Florida, in a quaint white silk gown cut low on the shoulders, and wearing a cluster of violets among the coils of her smooth brown hair. Her lids were downcast. She walked slowly, with unstudied grace, and she was as self-forgetful as if there had not been an eye to follow her movements. As it was, however, every glance was riveted upon her, owing to a certain magnetic, compelling power which it was hers always to exert. St. John purposely found a chair near which no one was seated; a word would have jarred upon him, perhaps broken the spell.

And it seemed to him that suddenly the room had taken on a strange new brilliancy—a touch of mystery, of poetic grace which, an instant before, the scene had wholly lacked. There was that about her which thrilled him like the sight of some perfect, solitary bloom on a sterile mountain height. She was so utterly apart, so different from all the rest, so alone, and so beautiful in her sad isolation. He longed to speak to her, to reach out both of his hands to her, and in a rush of tenderness, untinctured by a thought but that of human sympathy, to say: "I, too, have endured it all; I understand." He felt irresistibly drawn to her through the kinship of a like experience in pain; for he intuitively knew that upon her, beyond whatever of actual sorrow she had known, the mere pressure of life had heavily weighed.

He waited with some curiosity for the song she should select. He recalled the capabilities of her voice; and it was an opportunity.

Her hands ran aimlessly over the keys. She hesitated a moment, then threw a warm, brief glance across the room to where her father sat with his eyes upon her.

It was the quietest of quiet little songs that Florida sang, and it was evident to St. John, from the first, that she was singing, entirely regardless of effect— and for one. And though they cannot in any way convey the impression that was made, the words may be given here for the sake of their own simple, long-forgotten beauty:

> "On the lake where drooped the willow,
> Long time ago,
> Where the rock threw back the billow
> Curled liquid snow,
>
> "Dwelt a maid beloved and cherished
> By high and low;
> But alas, too soon she perished,
> Long time ago.
>
> "Rock and tree and flowing water,
> Long time ago,
> Bird and bee and blossom taught her,
> Love's spell to know.
>
> "There we met and loved and parted,
> Long time ago,
> There I lingered, broken-hearted;
> Tears, let them flow.
>
> "To her grave they're sadly given,
> Where flow'rets blow;
> She's the star I missed from heaven,
> Long time ago."

For some time after the song had ceased, and the hum of conversation had begun, the thrall of that pathetic "long time ago," with all of its far suggestiveness, held him still. St. John felt in no mood for conversation, and accordingly he remained where he was — in a recess, shielded by a portière—bending inattentively, and by way of apology merely, over an illustrated volume on the table at his side.

Presently he was roused from the mood that possessed him by Mrs. Alexander's impatient voice near by, as she swept hurriedly past.

"Where did you put them, Florida? Oh, in that cabinet, over there? What was your idea for such careful concealment? I want you to take the one giving a side view to Judge Overton. He has just been saying that to-day I am the one woman in Kentucky who can boast an absolutely perfect profile, and lamenting the fact that Joel T. Hart no longer lives. He spoke of it just after you had finished singing, my dear. And now that I think of it," she broke off, suddenly lifting her superb head from above the bric-à-brac through which she had been nervously rummaging, "let me ask what ever possessed you to select that song?—so absurdly monotonous. If ever I attempt another musical!''

At this moment, having found the object of her search—a package of her latest photographs—she turned suddenly, and espied St. John.

''Ah!'' she exclaimed, with frigidity; ''so this is your way of making yourself agreeable, is it, Mr. St. John?''

The young man's dark face flushed hotly at her tone. He had scarcely heard her words. His eyes were fixed in an eager scrutiny upon the younger woman's changeful countenance. Florida was standing quite at his elbow, and she drew back, a little startled, from his close proximity.

''Wait a moment, my dear.'' Mrs. Alexander placed a firm hand upon the girl's wrist. ''There is no hurry about the picture. I suppose I must make you two young people acquainted,'' and she went through the form of introduction as if lending herself to an act altogether beneath her.

"Florida, you have probably heard of Mr. St. John," she added with supercilious suavity. "He has written some sweet little verses; you may have seen them in the magazines."

A look of pained surprise traced itself upon her stepdaughter's features. Florida opened her lips to speak, evidently with some intention to try to do away with the effect of a discourtesy offered to one really distinguished, hesitated an instant, and then in silence lifted her eyes impulsively, beseechingly, to his, only to meet his absorbed, half-amused, wholly comprehending gaze.

VI

"I'm sorry she ever came back, that's what I am; aren't you, Ethel?"

"Are you, Louise? I don't know. Why?" The speaker, a little brown creature with thin, peaked features, pushed back the long hair from about her face, and looked up, meditatively, for a moment, from the fascinations of one of the Duchess' novels. "Why are you sorry, Louise?" she repeated vaguely.

"Oh, because I am, you stupid," replied the elder girl sharply; "and you'd be, too, if you knew all I know," with an air of superiority. "You didn't hear her telling on us to mama, as I did, the other day. I was listening at the key-hole, and I heard every word."

"Oh, Louise! *What* did she tell?" The child had begun to tremble violently, the recollection of her misdeeds evidently weighing heavily upon her conscience. "Did she say anything about me reading the Duchess?"

"Yes, she did," returned Louise, slowly shaking her head, and eyeing the culprit with a solemn stare. "She said she thought it was just *awful* in mama to let you read such things. When I am a young lady I hope I won't be like Florida," she declared. "I shan't care for anything but beaux and diamonds," with a simper and toss of the head. "She actually asked mama to let her teach us a little while every day this summer. Now, wasn't that just the meanest thing you ever heard of? How would she like to go to school all winter and summer, too?"

"*What* did mama say?" cried Ethel, aghast. The two children were in the garden, seated on a wooden bench under the arbor.

Louise waited several moments, teasingly, before she deigned to reply.

"Mama said," she began, finding an obvious delight in prolonging the agony of suspense, and holding a grape leaf before her eyes to watch the effect of the sunlight upon it,—"I wonder if we shall have many grapes this year; I just love grapes, don't you, Ethel?"

"Oh, Louise, what did mama say?" Tears had gathered in the dark eyes, and the meager little form was quivering with intense anxiety. "Won't Florida ever let us have anything more to eat? And if she teaches us, do you think she will beat us every day?"

"Mama said," pronouncing the words with slow distinctness, and with a remarkable mimicry of voice and manner, "she said, 'For pity's sake, Florida, leave the children alone. I forbid you,'— those were mama's own words—'I must positively forbid you to practice any of your the—the—theryries upon them."

"Then you are a hateful, horrid thing to come here bothering me and scaring me half to death," exclaimed Ethel, with an angry stamp of the foot, as she returned to her book. "Go away, right this minute; I want to read. He's just going to propose."

"Propose indeed! What do you know about proposing, a baby like you? How old are you, missy, anyway, I'd like to know?"

The tiny being lifted her eyes in quite serious surprise. "Louise," said she, gravely, "that's a very impolite question; some people don't like to tell their age. Besides, I wish you'd go away, you make my head ache."

"*Your* head ache! You're too *young* to have the headache," flouted the other, with a curl of the lip. "I've just begun to have the headache myself," and with this utterly crushing rejoinder she arose with much dignity and marched grandly into the house, pausing, however, when her foot was on the doorstep to throw back a mocking little laugh in the direction of the grape-arbor. "Your head ache! Little bit o' thing just ten years old!"

This amiable conversation between her two little half-sisters, painfully revealing their disposition toward herself, floated up to Florida where she lay, one warm afternoon, in a hammock on the balcony outside her bedroom. She was wide awake in an instant, stung to the heart by their childish, unpremeditated cruelty. Suddenly she rose and walked quickly to the balustrade, thinking to call the children to her. But she checked the impulse. She went back and sat down, putting her hand to her head, as if in pain.

"I ought not—oh, I ought never to have come back here!" she said to herself with a sob. "It all seems such a wasted effort. There is no place for me." But in another instant a passion of unselfish regret had swept over her. "Poor little misguided ones," she cried within herself, "and if only I might help them—if only she would *let* me help them!" feeling her woman's nature stirred with a yearning pity and love.

And this incident, trivial as ordinarily it might have appeared, contained for her a mournful and impressive meaning. What was it possible for her to make of her life here? Thus the old disturbing questionings as to duty and responsibility were roused anew, and a fuller recognition of her soul's great needs was thrust upon her. Wearied of all the world had to offer as far as her own life was concerned, yet hearing no longer the call to go and work among the unfortunate ones of the earth, she had come back at last to this that she called her home, asking only for the meagerest share in its daily hopes and interests, and ready to give her all in return; but she had felt herself so strangely apart, so inharmonious an element that it seemed wholly impossible to make herself understood.

She lay for some moments in her hammock, flushed and ill at ease. Instead of the dumb apathy that had been over her of late, all her former restlessness was revived, but modified in its effect, since there appeared to be before her only the prospect of a weary waste of years; and feeling the absolute necessity for movement, activity in any form, she realized that she was caged, bound hand and foot. The golden afternoon was no longer beautiful to her, the flower-scented air was sickening and oppressive. She rose and went into her bedchamber, and removing the thin, airy garment she wore, dressed herself in an outdoor costume.

A few minutes afterward she was out of the house, walking, with no particular destination in view, up the shaded street.

Not too far away, in this direction, and just outside of the town, there was a dim old woods where she had spent many afternoons since her return. She had just decided that she would go there for an hour's quiet, taking the electric car at the corner, and walking the remainder of the way, when her sensitive ear caught the sound of a voice far away in the distance—a voice so sweet and musical and wholesome that she involuntarily paused and waited for it to come nearer.

It proved to be the voice of a boy of ten or eleven years, as ragged and unkempt an urchin as one is likely to see; but a "bonnie laddie" he was withal, she saw as he approached, for there was a gleam of gold in the curling brown hair and a wistful look in the violet eyes that went straight to the heart. He was singing a cheap little air caught up from the streets, yet in such delicious tune, in such spontaneous overflow of joy as was simply irresistible.

Under one arm he carried a small bundle of newspapers, having disposed of all but three. At the sight of Florida and the intimation of a possible purchaser, he suddenly broke off in his singing, the clear, ringing voice calling forth in the most business-like and matter-of-fact tones.

"Couri*ay* Journal—*In*quire—Commer-*shul*! *All* about the fight! Big railroad wreck! Five lives lost! Fourteen crippled——''

"Will you sell them all to me?" asked Florida, cutting short the deafening appeal, and motioning in the direction of the papers.

The boy came to an abrupt stand-still. He regarded her a trifle suspiciously for a moment, and then replied, laconically, and with an air of indifference:

"Sell 'em to you ef you wants 'em."

"I do want them," answered Miss Alexander, sweetly, opening her purse and watching the saucy little face with interest. "I think I shall be glad to buy one from you every day if you will be so good as to give me the opportunity. But you will have to tell me your name, so that in the future I shall be able to distinguish you from others of your profession. Would you object to telling me your name?"

"Named Tim," was the brief response.

"Ah, Tim, is it?" exclaimed Florida,

bestowing a radiant smile upon the little fellow. "Do you know, Tim, I have always thought that a very sweet name? I can't recall that I have ever known any one whose name was Tim before," reflectively; "but I do like it, very much indeed."

The youngster made no reply. He seated himself upon the curbstone, evidently feeling that his work of the day was over, having disposed of the last of his papers, and taking from his pocket a large, red, juicy apple, he proceeded to devour it with avidity, manifesting about as much recognition of his interrogator's presence as a Hindu idol is in the habit of bestowing upon its votaries.

"Is Tim the only name you have?" inquired Miss Alexander, presently. She was leaning against one of the maples that lined the sidewalk, and there was a half-playful, half-serious look in her eyes. "Is Tim your only name?" she asked persuasively.

"Twine," was the oracular response.

Miss Alexander nodded. "Timothy Twine it is, then, in full," said she, smiling still. "And do you know, Mr. Timothy Twine, you have one of the most beautiful voices that was ever heard? How should you like—" She hesitated a moment before making the proposition, seeming in the next instant to arrive at a quick decision; "how should you like to come to me for a short while every afternoon for a little study in music and—and other things? I should so much like to have you. Will you come?"

"Dunno." Then after a pause in which the young gentleman had well-nigh choked himself into a fit from a too-bountiful bite of apple, he slowly turned his eyes toward her. "You better lookin'," he admitted, after a prolonged scrutiny, "than t 'other one."

"T 'other one?" suggested Miss Alexander gravely.

"The long-nosed one."

"Oh," Florida hastened to declare, "I should hope so. I never did like long-nosed people myself; Tim, I'm like you in that. Do you know, I think we are going to be very good friends, indeed. Tell me now, what is *your* chief objection to long-nosed people?''

''They 's too meddlesome.''

Miss Alexander winced a little under this rather pointed thrust.

''And was that the fault of 't 'other one'? Was she inclined to be meddle-some also?''

''You bet! Geewhilikins, wuzn't she er stunner!'' He swallowed the last piece of his apple, core and seeds and stem and all, and straightening himself up with an expression of deep inward satisfaction, he philosophically resigned himself to the enforced conversation.

''She had right smart pimples on her face,'' he volunteered, ''an' her hair wuz kinder black an' kinky. She wuz a sight taller 'n you air. She wore specs.''

''*Did* she, Tim?'' inquired Florida, with sympathetic interest. ''But you know she should not be judged too harshly for that; she may have had weak eyes. As for her nose—I can't help holding her just a little responsible for her nose, if it's all you say of it; I resent it as a personal affront. But what did she do to you?"

"She tuk me down to er church, an' they put er long white shut on me, an' had me a-singin' in the choir long with the rest, an'——"

"Oh, I understand. But my plans for you were of a different and much less pious description. I am not in any way connected with choir boys myself, so you see the lady with the long nose and pimply countenance was a far more serious and worthy individual, after all. I merely thought to give you a little musical training that would be helpful to you in the years to come; for you are going to be one of the great singers of the world, Tim, there cannot be the smallest doubt of that, and I felt a selfish longing to go down to fame 'on the hem of your garments,' so to speak—as Sir Joshua Reynolds remarked after he had painted the portrait of Mrs. Siddons.''

Unable to appreciate more than a word or two of this airy flight, Tim's glance again took on the look of mistrust it had worn when she had insisted upon purchasing all of his papers.

"And I thought," she continued, "that you might not find it altogether tiresome to make me this little visit every day, on account of the cherries, and the strawberries and the peaches and the grapes that grow at the place where I live. You may have just as much of everything as you possibly can eat, Tim, for the sake of that lovely voice of yours.''

The boy's eyes seemed starting out of his head. "Who you be?" he finally blurted out, in a kind of reverential awe.

An expression of deep sadness traced itself upon Miss Alexander's features. "I don't know, Tim," she replied, very humbly. "I don't think I'm anybody when it comes to that. Sometimes I think there is just one word to describe me; but it is not a very pretty word, and it is *failure*. Perhaps, if you will come, by and by there will be some other word —a better and more hopeful word for me. At all events, I assure you I have not misrepresented things in the least; the cherries and the strawberries and the peaches and the grapes are all there, or will be there, and they are waiting for you.''

The rapture that beamed from the small, eager face was a joy to see. And even now she seemed to experience a foretaste of the warmth that was to come into her heart through contact with the life of a trustful little child; for there crept a sweet, gentle look into her eyes, and she dropped the slightly bantering and bewildering tone in her speech.

''Then you will come, Tim?'' she said, softly.

''I'll have to ask pap fust. Gimini! don't I hope he'll lemme!''

''Let's go and ask him now. Is it very far away?''

"'Tain't fur. Right 'round yender on Georgetown street, next doo' to the saloon."

"But won't he be at work at this hour of the day?"

"Pap don't do no work," replied the child, loftily. "Leastways, he don't do much, 'ceptin' drivin' a dump-cart oncet in a while, when he gits ready."

It was obvious that Mr. Timothy Twine the elder was the gentleman of elegant leisure that his son had described, for he was found seated upon the wooden doorstep of his ramshackle abode adjoining the corner grocery, smoking a pipe of peace, his bland countenance unruffled by a care. He stumbled awkwardly to his feet, being somewhat afflicted with rheumatism, as Miss Alexander and his boy approached. A sly twinkle shone in his eye.

"Mr. Twine," said the young lady, quite simply, "I have come to ask you to lend me Tim for a little while every afternoon; I want to teach him something of music. And I shall consider it a kindness if you will let him come. He is very eager for your permission."

Mr. Twine's broad countenance relaxed still further in a grin of fond, paternal pride.

"Tim's powerful pop'lar," he declared, with a wink; "powerful pop'lar. There wuz another un here after him no more'n six weeks ago."

"So he has told me," assented Miss Alexander. "He has really a most beautiful voice, and it should be managed with the utmost care. For the present, I had thought of giving him lessons on the piano, if you have no objection to the plan."

Mr. Twine seemed unable to grapple with so important a question standing, so he again seated himself upon the doorstep. He appeared to be slowly revolving the idea in his mind. Presently he looked up. "The jews'-harp makes mighty prutty music," he remarked, confidentially, at length; "mighty prutty music. Ef I could afford it, I'd have one all the time.''

At the suggestion of such reckless expenditure, Miss Alexander kept an embarrassed silence.

''Then Tim may begin his lessons tomorrow afternoon?'' she said finally. ''I thank you very much for allowing him to come. I live not very far from here. I am Miss Alexander—Major Alexander's daughter; you may know the name.''

''Know the name? Bless my soul! The ole Major's darter, did ye say? Bless my soul! Well, I jes' reckon I do know the ole Major—fin'st ole gentleman in the State o' Kentucky, or anywheres else, fur the matter o' that. The ole Major! Why he can't be beat by *nobody*,'' said Mr. Twine, waxing more and more eloquent as he went along, after the fashion of Kentucky orators. ''Me an' him's great friends. *Been* friends nigh onto twenty year. Time an' agin, when he's seen me a-reelin' long kinder off like, Miss, he's put his han' on my shoulder right firm like, an' he sez: 'Tim,' sez he, *you will kill yourself* ef you don't leave off a-frequentin' of the dram-shop, ez you air a-doin',' sez he. But Lord, Miss, 'twan't nothin' but beer. The ole Major's ez innercent ez a lam'; he wuz thinkin' of ole Bourbon; but 'twan't nothin' but beer."

Not feeling herself capable of doing full justice to this distinction, Florida wisely brought the interview to an end.

And so, with little Tim, there had come a new element into her life, and existence seemed no longer an altogether empty thing.

VII

And May had come at last!

All the long winter in his wanderings through the brown woods St. John had found himself looking forward to the coming of spring under the soft Kentucky skies with especial anticipation. On many portions of the globe he had waited for her return, stretching forth the eager arms of a lover to receive her, and feeling his heart warm and thrill in her presence with profoundest joy. But something had caused him to believe that this time her advent would be different from any other. For miles around he knew the country with the precision that comes from the habit of close and studious observation, the exactness of the trained eye and ear of the practiced writer. And his reward had been to hear the first song of the bluebird and the robin, and one day down by the willows to catch an early "halcyon note" above the cold gurgle of the stream as the kingfisher, like a cerulean flash, darted across the brook. "Now surely, we shall have fine weather!" he had said to himself in almost boyish glee, recalling the pretty old legend of the bird. But the winter had been bleak for Kentucky, and March had been even more boisterous than March generally is, and April of most uncertain mood; so that it was not until May had been fully ushered in that he felt safe in abandoning himself to a secure delight. However, one learns to wait.

One brilliant morning near the middle of the month he came and stood in his doorway, looking out upon a street rustling in cool, green silken garments and vocal with the singing of birds and the shouts of happy children at play.

Opposite, what promised to be a somewhat imposing structure was in process of erection. The workmen called cheerily

to each other as they went about their al-
lotted tasks. One, standing on a long
ladder high above the heads of all the
rest, broke forth, from time to time, into
snatches of a song, yet never pausing an
instant in his work.

> "I look away across the sea
> Where mansions are prepared for me,"

sang the man in a voice quavering and
broken, but with now and then a note of
rare sweetness, just as an old worn-out
instrument will sometimes emit pleasant
sounds solely because of the music that
is in the heart of the player.

With a touching significance the voice
floated down to St. John where he stood
idly surveying a display of energies which
he felt in no way disposed to emulate.

The street, which was long and well-
shaded throughout, was regarded as an
attractive drive, and this morning it was
thronged with coupés, carts, victorias—
vehicles of every kind. Their occupants
basked in the genial sunshine, and lent an
air of festivity to the scene by their crisp,

fresh toilets, being suggestive of huge nosegays borne gayly past. All Lexington appeared to be on wheels, and to be moving by his door. Now and again from beneath a gauzy parasol or wide, flower-bedecked hat there was a smile and gracious bow in his direction. No one seemed to be going anywhere, he observed, or to have the smallest object in view beyond a sensuous indulgence in the mere joys of living. And some of their charming irresponsibility must have communicated itself to him, also, with demoralizing effect; for while he was debating as to how he should best employ his time, it being a Saturday morning, suddenly there awoke in him a spirit of revolt, and he decided at once, and with emphasis, that as for him, he, too, would do no more work that day of any kind—no, not so much as the writing down of a single line of verse, simply because the sun shone so and the whole earth seemed so glad.

Presently, with the expression of one

about to yield to temptation, he let his glance wander far down the street in the direction of the Alexander mansion. Its tall, white columns were barely to be discerned through the trees. Since the musical he had called repeatedly. He was, therefore, at some difficulty to persuade himself that it was highly proper he should present himself there again on this particular morning; yet he did very much wish to go.

From the first he had been ready to admit that he found Miss Alexander something more than interesting. Many people were that; she was more. He could have wished at times that she would meet him a little less frankly—with an occasional dash of coquetry or self-consciousness, perhaps; but she was never self-conscious with him in the least.

He had hoped that they might be friends, picturing to himself the future delights of such companionship—he who lent himself so sparingly to association with his fellow-beings, less perhaps on account of a lack in warmth of nature than because of a constitutional constraint.

Always most cordial, most kind, when she turned her great sad eyes upon him, he felt as if she were looking at him from a long way off, and without recognition. And though, with infinite tact—never however, having actually dwelt upon the subject of his work—she had caused him to feel that she respected what he had done, yet to him as the individual aside from the author he could not flatter himself into believing that she had given the briefest thought.

But the passionate reserve of his own nature respected the proud reticence of hers, and the strange isolation in which she chose to veil herself rendered her peculiarly alluring; for Mystery is always twin-sister to Charm, if they be not one and the same.

In temperament they were totally unlike; with him repression was inherent; with her it had been developed through circumstances. But she was not without

Florida Alexander

occasional swift, daring impulses which
sometimes thrust all barriers aside, giving
her imprisoned soul the wing; and she
was far from being habitually *triste*. On
the contrary, he noted that she had
moods of impetuous expression, when
her speech was brilliant and her countenance illumined with the flash of unre-
strained thought; furthermore, she possessed a rare sense of humor, lending
herself to mirth with a gayety, feverish
and spasmodic it is true, but in a manner
irresistible. It was only when her face was
in repose and she had withdrawn again
into herself that one recognized upon her
features the imprint of a sadness unspeakable, as of some fatal, haunting remembrance.

It suddenly came to St. John, looking
longingly in the direction of her abode,
that he still retained several rare old volumes of early Kentucky history kindly
lent him by the Major, and he decided
that this was a most fitting occasion to
return unto that gentleman his own. He

accordingly departed with alacrity into the house, appearing a few moments afterward with half a dozen time-worn volumes (which, however, he guarded most carefully, knowing well their priceless value) under his arm.

He would ask for the Major, he decided, as he proceeded down the street, no one else, adding that he had come to return some books. And Fortune might be kind; at all events, he would present himself as a humble suppliant for her favor.

He found the Major in his library, standing with his back to the door, and just about to take a beloved volume from one of the bookshelves.

The aged colored man that announced St. John coughed behind his hand in respectful hesitation, being evidently of the opinion that the call was inopportune; nevertheless, desirous of maintaining the hospitable record of the house, he threw wide the heavy oaken door, ushering in the visitor with especial stateliness

as a mark of his own private consideration.

"Eh?" inquired the Major, absently,
without lifting his head from his book,
the pages of which he was slowly scan-
ning in search of a favorite passage.
"Eh? What is it, Abram?"

"Pardon the interruption, Major," said
St. John, advancing in some embarrassment; "I——"

The Major, slightly bewildered, turned,
adjusted his spectacles, and perceiving
St. John, came forward with outstretched
hand.

"Ah, is it you, my young friend?" he
exclaimed, heartily. "This is kind, very
kind. Have that chair," indicating the
one in which he himself was accustomed
to sit.

"I will sit here, thank you, Major," replied St. John, taking the nearest seat.
"I can remain only for a moment. I
came to return these books, and I am
afraid that I have rather trespassed upon
your kindness in keeping them so long."

Florida Alexander

The Major waved his hand. "My library is always at your disposal, sir. Never hesitate to make use of it as if it were your own."

"I have found the study of the early history of the State as presented by these authorities delightfully entertaining," St. John began, having expressed his grateful appreciation of this courtesy. "There can be no question that the first settlers were a most remarkable people."

The Major's countenance glowed with the pride of a true Kentuckian.

"Ah, Mr. St. John," he said, "if I mistake not, as you continue your studies you will find ample justification of the praises that have been bestowed upon this people. But how few are the names that are imperishable! New leaders will appear to dim the remembrance of Kentucky's abler sons, and in the great party strifes 'our children's children will raise new idols, and cavil where their sires adored.'" He spoke under the stress of a profound emotion.

St. John was silent for a moment, and then said, very gently: "I feel that I have never been able to express to you my gratitude for the aid you have given me through our conversations on these subjects. There are a number of things in connection with the pioneer period, especially, upon which I should like to have your opinions," he continued. "And some time when you are in the mood for imparting them, I should be glad to have your views in regard to the mounds of this section," adding, by way of throwing off the discussion for the time, "That is an interesting suggestion offered by some that this town is built upon the site of an ancient walled city."

A merry twinkle crept into the Major's eyes, and the corners of his mouth twitched.

"I think," said he, at length, with a quiet smile, "that some of my ancestors would have felt disposed to answer those learned gentlemen you speak of somewhat in the fashion of old Edie Ochiltree's reply to the Antiquary. The latter was eloquently disclosing to young Lovel his discovery of the exact local situation of the final conflict between Agricola and the Caledonians, pointing out the site of the Praetorium of the Roman camp. 'Prætorian here, Prætorian there,' said old Edie, who had suddenly appeared upon the scene. 'I mind the bigging o't.' "

It was evident, for that day at least, that the Major was not disposed to treat the matter seriously, and fearing that he had already stayed too long, St. John arose a few moments afterward to take his departure, the Major insisting that he should remain, yet unable, however, to restrain a covert glance from time to time in the direction of "The Excursion," lying temptingly near on the table.

But just as he was leaving, unexpectedly, the opportunity St. John had hoped for was bestowed. The Major crossed the room, and throwing open a glass door leading by a flight of steps into the garden, said pleasantly:

Florida Alexander

"You will find my daughter out there among the roses. If an old man cannot interest you this bright day——"

And so quite easily it had come about that St. John found himself an instant afterward walking down the long gravel path precisely in the direction he desired, his heart-beats quickening with every step, and the breath of myriad flowers rousing his senses to a tumultuous fancy.

She was seated under a wide-spreading elm almost as large as that described as having furnished a council hall for the "Colony of Transylvania in America," the first legislative body ever assembled west of the Alleghanies.

Saturated as he was with the old stories in the romantic history of the State, already he had begun to invest her with something of their remote picturesqueness, while the author in him presented her vigorous young womanhood as a fitting type for a poetic narration of those by-gone days. Throwing his thoughts backward a hundred years and more, and

with many a delicate touch of form and
color, in his imagination he conceived of
her as one of that band of heroic women
at Bryan's Station, who, in order to render it possible to resist the siege,
marched valiantly to the spring for water
within the rifle shot of six hundred Indian
warriors. Or, might she not, under similar circumstances, have been capable of
some such daring deed as that of that loving one who unbarred the gate of the fort
for the wounded young hunter pursued
by savages, only to receive her lover dead
in her embrace? He could readily picture her as one of the wives or sisters or
sweethearts of those days, molding the
bullets for the rifles of the men, caring
for their wounds, sharing their every peril
and hardship—perhaps as one of the
widows mourning the hideous slaughter of
the Blue Licks, and yet laying aside her
grief to buckle on the armor of her aveng-
ing friends.

Some lines of one of the early poets in

the State began to sing to him as he drew nearer:

"The mothers of our forest land
  Their bosoms pillowed men;
And proud were they by such to stand
  In hammock, fort, or glen,
To load the sure old rifle,
  To run the leaden ball,
To watch a battling husband's place,
  And fill it, should he fall. "

And as he looked at her now, the finished product of an advanced civilization, manifesting in her bearing the self-poise of the college-bred woman and the accomplished grace that comes of a luxurious living, he realized that much of her romantic attraction for him lay in the knowledge that there flowed in her veins the blood of such women; and he intuitively felt that she must be all the braver and sweeter and truer because they had lived and loved and suffered and died so many long years before.

Not a detail in her appearance escaped him to-day, and he saw that she was charming in a white lawn gown, a black

Florida Alexander

Gainsborough hat with plumes, and a
light silk shawl of a bird's-egg blue
thrown loosely about her shoulders. She
was reading, apparently with absorbing
interest, a book which she thrust a little
hurriedly aside when she looked up suddenly to find him standing within a few
yards of her.

"Ah—you?" she cried, a trifle disconcerted for an instant, yet flashing a
warm, welcoming smile upon him. "You
must have borrowed Siegfried's cloud-
cloak."

He noted that the pomegranate glow
in her cheeks was heightened, and that
there was a sparkle in her eyes as if the
glory over the earth had thrilled her to a
passionate forgetfulness of self. Never
had he seen her in precisely such a mood.
He came forward with an eagerness that
contrasted strangely with his customary
formality.

"Did he get tired of you?" Florida
asked, gayly, as she rose, holding out her
hand in quite friendly greeting.

Florida Alexander

"I am very much afraid that he did," answered St. John, meekly, taking the rustic chair she offered.

"But you should appreciate the discrimination he makes in your favor. Perhaps you do not know that you belong to a most despised guild?"

"Oh, yes," he replied, "I do know. I have known it for some time."

"Then you have been made to realize that it is no light matter to answer to the offense of being a modern author. However, he seems ready to allow you a special dispensation."

With seeming carelessness her hand sought the book she had been reading, thrusting it more securely out of sight among the folds of her shawl, which had dropped from her shoulders.

"I am never quite able to decide," continued she, "which he holds in the greater contempt, the writers of most of our recent literature, or the readers; and to read, therefore, what is written is according to him to become a *particeps criminis*, without even the poor excuse in one's favor of winning a livelihood thereby.''

"Oh, as to the livelihood——" put in St. John, with a laugh and a shrug of his shoulders.

But she went on in the same light tone, throwing a playful, lustrous glance toward him, and lending herself in a kind of reckless abandon to the first subject that offered:

"In our efforts to extricate a thought out of much that is written, he says that we remind him of a lot of hungry dogs snatching at a bone withheld always by a teasing hand; and that, if by especial dexterity one of us succeeds, or thinks he succeeds, in grasping the thought— that is, the bone—we generally find to our mortification on closer scrutiny that it is not really a bone after all, but only a pithless piece of painted chalk.''

St. John's smiling appreciation of this was a base disloyalty to the "despised guild" and to his own convictions.

"We should at least be grateful for our illusions," he said, unable to conceal in his expression the delight that her presence afforded.

The wind stirred the tendrils of polished brown hair drawn smoothly back from her low brow. What a picture she was! all grace and fire and womanliness, with that touch of airy raillery to-day that had heretofore been lacking. He was grateful for that; it made him feel as if they were becoming a little better acquainted, as if one tiny corner of the veil had been lifted and she was peering out at him with amused interest.

"He may be quite right about it," the rich voice persisted, in evident enjoyment of the subject, "so far as regards fiction, that is," with a mocking little smile and a nod, "that old romantic school of his is certainly delightful. And there is so much in this modern realism that revolts. It is difficult to say just wherein our artists blunder."

"I think," replied St. John, quite seriously, the teacher habit asserting itself for the moment, with a certain inherent force that usually characterized his speech, "I think the blunder comes mainly from the fact that so many novelists fail to recognize, or refuse to recognize, one thing: simply that the ideal is the real."

She smiled a little at his unconsciously didactic tone, her thoughts wandering away to his own pure verse—a lofty, impassioned tribute to the Ideal, as expressed in nature and in humanity, before whose shrine he continually worshiped.

"It is necessary to keep this before one always," he insisted, "as well as that other truth that a perfect art *must* involve a perfect morality."

The breeze swept some rose leaves to her from a near trellis. She smoothed the delicate petals against her pink palm for a moment reflectively. When she lifted her head her manner was subdued, totally altered.

"But those works that exercise the

greatest influence over our subsequent actions are usually such as we feel no disposition to analyze. They may or may not reach the true standard, and seem to come as by a mere accident into our lives, like a flower wafted to the feet.''

''Ah, that is undoubtedly true,'' he assented, with comprehension.

''And the mood, the peculiar state of mind, that means so much.''

''So much.''

Her expression had returned to its old sadness, and it was evident that through the trend of ideas some deep undercurrent of feeling had been stirred. Her voice sank lower, faltered, broke. She seemed suddenly to have become wearied and cold; but she did not draw her shawl about her. When she spoke again, it was as if, swept on by an impetuous impulse, she was allowing him to know her inmost thoughts in a kind of sub-consciousness of his presence.

''Once a book came into my hands, by chance, as I then thought,'' she said, in low, hurried tones. "It was at a time in my life of responsibility and uncertainty and sleepless pain. One day I entered a shop in New York, and of the new books that were handed out to me I bought one at random, yet feeling in some vague way that it would contain a message for me. But having taken it home, the mood to read passed. For weeks it lay on my table, inviting me to open it, until I finally grew nervous under its silent entreaty. One especially dark day I took it up. I read on and on for hours. The thoughts in it burned into my brain and heart. They seemed to hold out the possibility of an existence purer and more spiritual, through a higher consecration to truth, than I had ever dreamed of. Long passages, entire pages even, clung to me, until my whole being was steeped in the delicate subtleties of the ideal interpretation—the interpretation of the poet, it is true, yet of the man also, cognizant of all human weakness and resisting it with his utmost strength. There was

something god-like in that clear flute-
note. And there came a time when the
exalted standard that had been offered
seemed beckoning to me always. I was
no longer tempted. The way was plain.
I thought—I thought I did what was
right. Who can ever know? The book
decided my destiny for me, that is all."

A convulsive shudder swept over her,
and a smoldering fire burned in the dark
eyes. She added quickly: "At no
other moment of my life could this book
have made anything approaching the impression that it did. Perhaps it was all a
mere superstitious fancy. But when I
went abroad I took it with me; I had
been reading it again this morning when
you came."

St. John's eyes wandered involuntarily
in the direction of where the book lay
concealed. He was silent, mystified,
saddened. He looked instantly away
again, beyond the roses and fruit-trees
and flowering shrubs, to where a fountain
splashed in the sunlight. Presently she

turned her face to him, pale, but perfectly controlled. Her lips parted in a
conventional smile.

"You must like it here—this pretty
old-time garden," she said, rather formally. "I am so glad that you should
have seen it on such a day."

He looked at her thoughtfully for a
moment. "It is beautiful —very beautiful," he replied, gravely.

She shrank a little from the pitying
tenderness in his eyes.

"I am like Walther von der Vogel-
weide," she said. "Do you not hate
it, too, the long winter? I love him for
all the hard things he has said of it—for
the birds and me."

"But even Walther forgave one winter
of his life—the winter of his happiness.
I can understand that."

"Walther was a mediæval poet."

"Every man is a poet that loves a
woman."

He had risen, and was looking down
upon her where she sat, his face lighted

with a sudden flame, and transformed with a new and sacred beauty. She reached nervously backward for her shawl, avoiding his glance, and in so doing the book she had been reading, being entangled, fell heavily to the ground, as suddenly she rose.

He leaned down to restore it, and she uttered a cry of protest, putting forth a swift, restraining hand. But she was too late. She drew back, white and trembling, something like terror creeping into her expression, while in a kind of trance-like, fascinated gaze she watched his alert movement.

As his glance fell upon the cover, he started, caught in his breath, and a hot flush mounted to his brow. He turned quickly toward her, and their eyes met —hers baffled and confused, his savagely triumphant.

The book was a copy of his own verse.

VIII

With a zeal that was highly commend-
able, if somewhat inconvenient, to his future instructress, Tim early presented
himself on the afternoon that was to
mark a strange turning in the existence
of this hitherto neglected little savage.
He was fully three-quarters of an hour in
advance of the time that had been agreed
upon, and Miss Alexander, who had been
roused from her nap by the reverberating
peal of his impetuous pull upon the door-
bell, was compelled to keep him waiting
some little while before she was able to
appear.

In sympathetic comprehension of the
child nature, she proceeded to array herself at once in one of her prettiest costumes for the occasion, a tea-gown of
peach-blossom colored China silk; and

she stood for a moment smiling gleefully back at her reflection in the long mirror of her bedroom after she was dressed.

When she finally went below, she found a small young person in the far end of the room looking decidedly abashed and uncomfortable. He was seated stiffly upon one of the gilt chairs, and his little bare legs were twisting and untwisting themselves about the rounds in a manner calculated to arouse a sensation of nervousness in the most phlegmatic. All his pertness of expression had disappeared, and a look of wide-eyed seriousness had so transformed the piquant countenance that for a moment Florida stood amazed. She was furthermore touched by the child's pathetic efforts at adornment as displayed in a cheap crimson necktie, long past its pristine freshness, and a dilapidated straw hat, many times too large, set rakishly back on the pretty curly head. Perhaps she would have felt the appeal even more had she known, which she did not, that to obtain at second hand

these polite adjuncts to his toilet he had
found it necessary to sacrifice three agates,
a kite and his well-beloved knife. Above
all, his face and hands were so alarmingly
clean, it was impossible not to experience
a certain uneasiness on witnessing such a
sudden and complete reform.

"Tim," she exclaimed, heartily, "I am
delighted to see you," taking the chair
at the boy's side, and bestowing one of
her slow, beautiful smiles upon him, a
smile that seemed to suggest the sunshine
and fruit and flowers and all lovely
things to the little fellow, for he gazed
dumbly into her face in a kind of rapt,
bewildered intoxication. "Did you have
any trouble in finding the place?" she
asked. "There is another house something like this farther down the street."

Tim appeared to be slowly recovering
the power of speech. He suddenly
straightened himself in his chair, gave an
odd little jerk to his shoulders, and broke
forth with the air of one about to relate
some thrilling and daring experience.

"Never had no trouble 't all," he declared, breathlessly. "Jest comed right along, an' walked up all them steps, an' rung the doo'-bell hard ez I could, an' that gentleman he comed an' let me in, an' I jest walked right in an' sot down in one them gold chairs, an'——"

"A gentleman, Tim?" inquired Miss Alexander, rather puzzled.

"Colored gentleman," remarked Tim, with a nod, thus incontestably proving that the blood of no slave-holding ancestor flowed in his veins.

"Oh, I see," replied Miss Alexander, amused. "It was Uncle Abram. And now I am so glad that we have made a beginning. Tim, dear, there is so much in making a beginning. I hope I am going to make you see that quite clearly, as well as so many other things. But I don't think I shall try to teach you very much to-day. We will just talk a little together and get acquainted. And in the first place I want to ask you what do you think is the reason why I so much wish you to study music, and have brought you here?"

Tim's face grew thoughtful. He leaned his elbows on his knees, and rested his chin in his hands. He seemed to be of the opinion that much depended upon the answer he should make.

"Give it up," he said at length, dejectedly, raising his head.

"Tim, I will tell you," Miss Alexander resumed, touching one of the crisp brown curls with a caressing movement and smiling still, in a kind of playful earnestness. "It is because you are one of those rare beings that help to flood this strange old world with light—in other words, you are a genius, Tim, and in my humble way I should like to fire the torch and assist in feeding the sacred flame. O Timothy," twisting the shining band of hair about her finger, "little dost thou dream what the gods shall yet require of thee."

Being as indifferent as one could be to the gift and nature of genius, and finding the new possession rather uncomfortable on the whole, Tim maintained an embarrassed silence. There was one and only one part of the remark that had the smallest interest or meaning for him; as his ear caught the word *feed*, he looked quickly up with a wink of appreciation, and Florida went on:

"It is the people that sing as you will one day, dear, that bear a most beautiful message to others. And I had the feeling, Tim, that as I have failed so sadly to do many of the kind and helpful things I had meant to do, perhaps some time after a great while you would speak for me, and so in this way that I would be no longer altogether dumb."

Tim's eyes began to wander about the room with eager curiosity. At this moment a servant entered and deposited a salver laden with eatables on a table near by. Miss Alexander rose. "Here are strawberries and buttered biscuits for you, Tim," she cried, bending above the tray. "Do you like strawberries and buttered biscuits?"

Florida Alexander

Tim was speechless with anticipation.

"And while you are eating them," she went on, gayly, "I will tell you a story of the time that is to come when you shall be a grown man, and the people will gather from far and near to hear you sing, and you will sing in the great operas, and perhaps you will be the mighty Siegfried himself, 'the far-renowned knight'; and I think I will tell you the story of Siegfried while you are eating your strawberries. But when you sing in the great opera the story will not be precisely as I tell it to you now; it will be something like it."

"Huccum 't won't?" inquired Tim, in one of his lapses into the negro dialect, arresting himself in the act of devouring an enormous strawberry, and slowly turning his eyes toward her.

"Oh, because it won't, Tim; never mind about that. Now, I'm going to begin. Long, long ago, far away over the seas, in a beautiful castle on the Rhine, there lived a mighty prince whose name was Siegfried. And this Siegfried was so strong, so very, very strong, there was no one in all the whole wide world that was a match for him, nor were there any wild beasts in the dark forests that he was afraid of in the least. And one day alone on the mountain he killed the terrible dragon, and bathed himself in the blood, and——''

Tim suddenly interrupted the narrative. Raising his small form with a gesture of infinite pride, he announced with flushed cheeks and flashing eyes:

"I ain't afeard o' *no*body, an' I ain't afeard o' *nothin'*."

Florida caught herself up with a start, realizing the drift of the story.

"No, Tim, no, of course not; of course you are not afraid," she said, rather nervously and hastily. "But you see the days in which the Prince Siegfried lived were very different days from our days, and what was courage in him might not be courage in one of us at all."

"Can't never let no nother boy jump on me."

"But for us it is courage *not* to fight— for us Kentuckians," Florida insisted, feeling that she had been rather unfortunate in her selection.

"Can't never let no nother boy jump on me," Tim stoutly maintained, by no means converted.

Miss Alexander looked disturbed; then a whimsical smile broke over her face, and she let her hands fall helplessly into her lap.

"Oh, Tim, Tim!" she exclaimed, with a laugh; "what a true son of Kentucky you are!"

But all at once her manner grew grave and sweet.

"Tim, dear," she said at length, "how am I ever going to make you see certain things, when your elders and your betters set you the example that they do?"

Her glance wandered away from the child, through the open window, far into the distance, until it reached the place out on the lawn where she and St. John had sat the day before. She was thinking of the explanation he had once offered of the fiery disposition of the Kentuckians. This he traced back to certain hereditary influences, holding that the spirit of resistance, essential to their forefathers— shut in as were the latter by the great wall of mountains on the one side and the waters on the other—while they struggled with the infuriated savages, had been transmitted, and that, naturally, a people accustomed to long years of such warfare would grow to look with less horror upon bloodshed than would others the conditions of whose development had been of a more peaceful character.

She recalled his manner, earnest, thoughtful, judicial, kindly—the varying expression in his deep blue eyes. She had thought them rather remarkable eyes. The entire impression came back to her, especially the feeling she had had once while he was speaking: the vivid realization that he unconsciously gave her of his own intense self-mastery, of his grasp upon the thought that the true fight is

within. And in sharp contradistinction
there flashed now, as then, before her
mind's eye, another face, a bold, reckless,
handsome face, startling her by the force
of the antithesis. Launcelot and Galahad!
Half-forgetful of the boy's presence, she
went softly over the lines that had begun
to hold a certain association in her
thoughts:

"My good blade carves the casques of men,
  My tough lance thrusteth sure,
My strength is as the strength of ten,
  Because my heart is pure."

Her eyes, presently traveling slowly
back to her well-contented little guest,
rested upon an empty plate; there was
absolutely not a crumb left, and she had
ordered, she thought, an absurdly bounti-
ful supply.

"Were you really so hungry, Tim?"
she asked, gently.

"Was right smart hongry," was the
reply.

"Do you think you could eat anything
more?" she hinted, not without some

inward misgivings as to the advisability of the proposition.

Tim hesitated. "Ef I wuz to stan' up an' go right slow—I think I mought," he finally confessed.

"I dare not, Tim, I *dare* not," Miss Alexander hastened to protest. "You surely would be ill. How long has it been since you had anything to eat?"

"Sence las' night."

"Last night! Are you often hungry —hungry as you were to-day?" Her face had grown very pitiful as she bent above him.

"Offen 'nough," he answered, briefly, drawing back a little from her caress. Presently he fixed his eyes intently upon her. "How many people could you feed?" he demanded most seriously.

"How many? Oh, I don't know, Tim; I never thought of it. Why do you ask?"

"Could you feed five thousand?" suggested Tim.

"Five thousand, Tim? I should never

think of attempting such a thing. The
idea is quite appalling. What do you
mean?"

Tim was silent a moment, and then
proceeded with much impressiveness.

"I hearn that somebody did oncet," he
declared. "With five loaves an'—an'"
—speaking with careful precision—"*with
five loaves an' two small fishes.*"

"Oh, but that was a miracle, Tim,"
responded Florida, reverently. "I did
not understand at first what you meant."

Tim's eyes were still fixed in a solemn
interrogation upon her face. After a
long pause, with the same soberness of
demeanor, "That never could ha' been,"
he asserted positively.

"It is all quite true, Tim," Florida
answered with equal firmness. "It is
none the less true because you cannot
understand."

Tim regarded her with the regretful
look of one who sees his idol about to
crumble at his feet. He was evidently

finding it rather difficult to comprehend that there could be such a thing as a similarity of teaching between the despised "long-nosed one," and this beautiful, resplendent creature who thrilled his little pagan heart with something nearer akin to a feeling of worship than he had ever known.

"All I got to say then," he said, at length, weakening in some small degree in his position, "they must ha' had a mighty little bit."

Florida reached forth an arm and drew the child closer to her. A great wave of tenderness, of compassion, of she scarce knew what, seemed to sweep over her, and to lend to her words a simple, direct beauty. In a low voice she began, smoothing with gentle touch the small brown head resting at her side as she told in language that he could understand the meaning of the heavenly bread, the mystery of the "meat which endureth unto everlasting life." And as she spoke, the shadows on the lawn grew deeper, and the sweet flower-laden air stole in through the windows, and the drowsy hum of insects kept up a pleasant monotone, until the little fellow felt a strange new sense of peace, his violet eyes opening and closing in a pretty, dreamy sort of way.

"And so, dear," she said, at last, and there was the throb of some inward pain in the quiet voice, "there are two things for us never to forget: to keep our own hearts pure, so that we may not choose the low things of the earth, and thus bring sorrow upon ourselves for all our days; and to try to be ready to give the true bread to others. There will be always many hungry ones. And though we cannot see the Kind Shepherd, as did the five thousand, and sometimes in our grief and blindness we may doubt His goodness even—it is so hard to see the dear God's face through our tears—we know that as He was sorry for them, He is sorry now for us, and does not wish that there should be any hungry ones, or discouraged, or sad."

The child suddenly raised himself and looked her long in the face. "You looks jest like er angel when you talks like that," he cried.

IX

On the outskirts of the town, not far
from the line of the street railway, there
was a dim old wood, almost as mysterious and as beautiful and as wildly som-
ber as were the first Kentucky forests that
broke upon the enraptured gaze of the
pioneers. The place bore an air of neglect, but a neglect altogether delightful in
its picturesqueness, being enclosed by a
vine-covered wall, crumbling here and
there, and affording to the wearied trav-
eler of the roadside such delicious glimpses
of cool retreats, such revelations in the
way of light and shade, undulation and
color as to send him on his way refreshed,
the redolence of the rank vegetation
steeping his senses into happy forgetfulness of heat and dust and blinding path.
St. John particularly delighted in the

spot, and when the warm June days cut
short his longer rambles into the country,
almost every afternoon found him here,
sometimes with notebook and pencil, as
often without, giving himself wholly up
to a profound and intimate communion,
which, when he afterward went to his
work, seemed in effect to breathe itself
into his writings, lending to them something of the uplifting power of nature
itself.

But recently his thoughts and the expression of them had taken an unaccus-
tomed turn; there had crept into his
verses a more distinctly human note, as if
his heart, hitherto closed to one feature
of the emotions in an intensity of reserve,
were now expanding under a sudden
warmth. It was with a quaint simplicity
that he yielded himself to the new influence. Self-centered, perhaps, because
of an over-zealous vigilance, loyal to
others, because true first to himself,
through this sway his nature seemed
likely to attain an elasticity which for-

merly it had lacked; for it is in experience and fulfillment that such a temperament reaches its height of development. And the difficult standard toward which he continually strove, the stature of the ideal man, had been complemented always by another standard—poetic, alluring, passionately pure—the stature of the ideal woman, before whose shadowy image he worshiped with something of the same fierce and enduring tenderness which of old Arthur enjoined upon his knights.

Two weeks had passed since that morning among the flowers, when he had felt that a new day was dawning for him. Though he had called repeatedly since that time he had not seen Miss Alexander once. It was characteristic of him that he did not attribute this circumstance to any impulse of coquetry in her, but continued to wait in calm trustfulness and patience for what he none the less ardently desired, though outwardly the longing was repressed.

When he did see her again, he came

upon her suddenly and quite by accident, finding her one afternoon in the depths of his favorite woods. She was seated on an old moss-covered log, and she wore a green wool gown and green straw hat, the colors melting so harmoniously into those about her that he was not conscious of her presence until he had drawn quite near. However, she recognized him some moments before he saw her. He was walking slowly, absorbed in thought, for to-day there had come a disturbing echo from the outside world; but at sight of her he uttered an exclamation of joyful surprise.

"Ah, what an unexpected pleasure to find you here!" he cried, coming quickly to her, a swift gleam lighting his dark face.

She returned his gaze in silence, smiling up at him in quiet greeting. For a moment there was a responsive flash in her eyes, but it changed instantly into an expression of merely friendly inquiry. With an air of proprietorship in her sur-

roundings which he found rather amusing in view of what he considered his own
claims of possession, she made a place for
him at her side.

"You *can't* know how glad I am to find
you here!" he repeated, warmly.

She slowly turned her face toward him,
and smiled again, this time in a rather
uncertain fashion.

"I am often here, when at home at
this time of the year," she replied. "But
I come generally in the morning, quite
early." She smoothed her glove, reflectively, between her fingers. "It is beautiful here at all times, but it is especially
beautiful in the morning, quite early,"
she said.

"At this moment it is perfect," answered St. John, simply and fervently,
adding with an effort at lightness: "Here,
I am among my friends; in June, with
Lowell, I am always ready to count 'a
tree among my far progenitors.'"

"Are you, too, often in these woods?"
inquired Florida.

"Very often. I doubt if the man that owns them does really own them after all. Some time I should like to compare notes and find out whether his pastures have ever yielded him as much as they have yielded me."

"You will have to ask her, not him; the land is owned by a woman, and if you ask her, and she is truthful, she will certainly answer no."

"Why do you make so sure of that?"

"Because I accept Plato's definition of a poet as 'a light and winged and holy thing;' the woman that owns this land is not a poet." She looked away, in the direction of the large red-brick structure in the distance, with a dreamy, intent expression in her eyes.

"The place has quite an ancient and historic suggestion," he said, following her glance. "But in Kentucky one never knows when he is upon sacred soil. Did I ever tell you of my Boonesborough experience?"

There was a ring in his voice of such

genuine joy in her presence, she avoided meeting his eyes. She shook her head, and he went on:

"In some way I had an incorrect idea; I was under the impression that Boones-borough was a large and thriving town. I especially wished to see the site of the old fort. One day last summer, when in my boat on the Kentucky River, knowing that I was somewhere in the neighborhood of the place, I called to a man who was ploughing on the hillside, and asked him to tell me how far I was from Boones-borough. The man regarded me stolidly for a moment, and then said:

" 'Stranger, ef ye'll git out o' thet thar boat, an' roll up them thar pants, ye'll be knee-deep in Boonesborough now.' "

Florida laughed. "At present you are knee-deep in nothing more notable than the far-famed bluegrass," she responded. "The house is not very old." Then she supplemented in a softened voice: "It was my mother's girlhood home. From a child I have haunted the spot. Did not the birds tell you?''

He turned and looked her quickly in the eyes.

''I can well believe now that they did,'' he said, quite earnestly, at length.

She flushed a little under his serious gaze, and hurried on. ''The place has been for six months without a tenant, but I shall rent it again in the autumn, I think. I so much dislike the idea of any one living in it, and it is only stern necessity that ever drives me to consider it. I have always a feeling that whatever of work and change existence may hold for me, some time I myself shall surely live in it; and I find my thoughts continually traveling onward to the time when, at the end of life, I shall come back here and take up my abode with only my silent companions—the ghosts of other days.''

He was still looking steadily at her, touched not so much by her words, which were spoken lightly enough, but by that undercurrent of pain which so often crept into her voice, and which her careless speech could not conceal. Her swift perception must have made her conscious of his pity, for in the next moment she strove to direct the conversation from herself.

"Were you composing a sonnet when you discovered me?" she inquired, cheerfully.

His expression underwent a sudden change. His face clouded, and he passed his hand wearily across his brow, as if recalling a disturbing thought, which, for the time, had been expelled by a happy interruption.

"No—no—it was not a sonnet," he answered, absently. "The fact is, I was not thinking of my work." He was silent a moment, and then all at once he turned abruptly toward her. "It might surely have been a dirge," he said. "Could you bear to have me tell you a little of myself, of the life before I came to this place?" he asked. "But it is not so much of my own life as of the life of some one who, for many years, was everything to me that I should like to speak, if you would care to listen.''

His manner was very quiet, but he was evidently stirred to the utmost depths of his nature by some thrilling recollection. His eyes were gravely earnest and he was paler than ordinarily. He waited for her reply.

She caught in her breath quickly, when she slowly lifted her eyes to his face. "If it is hard for you," she began, shrinking sensitively from she scarce knew what, "if it is hard——"

"Since my friend's death I have never been able to mention his name to any one; but it is not hard to speak of him to you," he said, with a profound sincerity in the words. "And to-day all my thoughts have been turned backward by a notice in one of the Eastern papers stating the death through consumption of the young girl to whom he had been engaged. It was of my friend I had been

thinking when I came upon you.'' The
hand that again swept across his brow
shook a little as he continued.

''We had been intimate since boyhood;
but it would be impossible to conceive of
two people more unlike. My life has
always been solitary; his was spent continually out in the world. Ardent, pleas-
ure-loving, wholly irresponsible, often
impulsively wrong, seldom deliberately
so, his was an organism in which, if there
was no pronounced tendency for good,
there was also no pronounced tendency
for evil; and in thinking of him, and of
the things he was led to do, it has always
been something to me to hold fast to the
thought that had he been less powerfully
tempted than he was he might some day
have become strong.''

She was leaning passively against the
bole of the massive oak at her back. Her
eyes were downcast, and her hands were
clasped rather tightly in her lap. She
appeared to be listening intently. Suddenly she half rose from her seat, and he

was startled by the sharp cry that escaped her. But in the next instant he perceived the cause of it; a rabbit had run across the path.

"Pardon me," said Florida, quickly, in a low voice. "I—I am not often so foolishly superstitious." A faint smile played about her lips. "Please go on," she insisted; her great brown eyes seemed filled with sympathetic interest. "You were saying that had your friend been less powerfully tempted than he was——"

"I had aways had the belief," resumed St. John, "that through the love of some good woman he might be made to see many things to which formerly he had been morally blind. But when one day he told me he was engaged to be married to a young woman I knew, I felt my heart sink with apprehension. The girl was pretty, but weak, wholly incapable of exercising the influence for which I hoped. My fears were only too soon realized; in less than three months I saw that he was growing cold in his feeling toward her.''

He was looking steadily away now, and he proceeded in a changed voice.

''But I did not fully realize the situation until the summer, when I knew that she had gone to Newport, and saw that he failed to follow her; and I do not think that he realized the situation at all. She wrote to him frequently—light, gossipy letters they must have been. He sometimes mentioned to me certain incidents of which she had written; we were very intimate. In her letters she made repeated, veiled references, withholding the name, to a beautiful young woman— from the South, I think—who must have been as magnetic and as alluring as she was beautiful; and it happened that the fanciful description caught his attention. As by accident, he carelessly touched upon the subject, from time to time, with me, and always there was something in his constrained, laughing tone to betray that he was strangely interested. It was scarcely a surprise to me when he finally announced his intention of going to Newport. He wrote to me one letter during the six weeks he spent there—the letter of a man blind, infatuated, utterly swept off his feet. Had this woman, who proved to be his destiny, been a good woman instead of the woman she was——''

She interrupted him with a sudden, sharp gesture. ''What right have you—how can you dare to lay all the blame upon her—upon this woman—whoever she may be?'' she cried. Her eyes were wide and staring, and her face was quivering with an intensity of feeling.

He turned toward her.

''It seems to me that there cannot be two opinions in the matter,'' he said, coldly. ''She understood the situation perfectly, knew that his highest allegiance was due another woman, a woman who was her friend, and knowing it, she proceeded to inflict the bitterest humiliation that one person can inflict upon another, and in the most public way. There is no limitation to the vanity of such a woman.''

She put up her hand to her throat and held it there for a moment.

''Have you no mercy?'' she implored. A shiver seemed to sweep over her. ''May she not have been powerfully tempted, too?'' The words broke from her at last in a despairing appeal.

He looked at her with admiration in his eyes. ''It is very beautiful that you should plead for her,'' he answered warmly; ''but you are so far incapable of such an act as hers as to be wholly unable to understand all that it implies.''

She drew back as if there had been that in his praise that stung.

''No; I have never been able to find the smallest excuse for her,'' he said, sternly, at length, ''for if at any time there was an excuse, her subsequent conduct left small room for doubt of her heartlessness. Having wrought all the mischief she could in the way of a broken engagement, and I may truly say a broken heart as well—for the death of the young girl to whom he had proved faithless really dated from that time—she seemed to take refuge in a cheap remorse. Refusing steadfastly to see him ever again, she went abroad, I think, and managed to hide herself from him for a time. He succeeded in finding her at length, however, and she informed him that she had somewhat misunderstood the nature of her feeling for him, imploring him to go back to the woman he had deserted. In a spirit of pique he did go back, and shortly afterward it was announced that the marriage would take place." He paused a moment, and then added: "Two weeks before the day fixed for the wedding he was drowned mysteriously off the coast——"

She turned wildly upon him. "It was an accident," she whispered, huskily, "surely it was that. I mean," suddenly checking herself, "what you imply is too hideous to be true. It must have been an accident," breathlessly. "Why—why—do you speak as if it were not?"

The corners of his mouth were compressed; evidently it was costing him a good deal to tell the story, even to her.

"It was not an accident," said St. John, slowly, at length. "He swam better than any one I ever saw; it is impossible that he could have been drowned, the circumstances being what they were. Moreover, I had proof."

He paused a moment and looked quickly about him. The woods had become darkened, and there was now and again a low, angry, rumbling sound, like the rage of a savage beast hungrily seeking its prey. The odor of the dank grasses was oppressive and the air was stifling. But Florida's eyes were still fixed upon his face in a kind of strained, breathless intentness. The supple figure had become rigid; her parted lips were dry and parched. Her eyes seemed to compel him to go on.

"A few moments before his death he

wrote a letter to me. It was the letter of a madman. There can be no question that, driven to desperation, he took his own life," he concluded, hoarsely. "Ballinger——"

Like a blade, a sudden, terrific flash of lightning cut off the unintentional mention of the name, and with a shriek Florida sprang trembling to her feet, as there followed a deafening, reverberating peal that seemed to shake the forest to its utmost depths.

He rose alarmed. With incredible rapidity the clouds had gathered. As frequently happens in Kentucky in the month of June, there had been but little warning, and it appeared now that the storm was about to break upon them in great fury.

He gave her a swift glance of uneasiness. She was still trembling, and very pale. The giant oak above them groaned and swayed. She stood as one stunned. "Come," he said, quickly, "we have not an instant to lose; come."

But she remained motionless, bewildered, her eyes still searching his face. "Come," he insisted again; but she seemed to shrink from him.

Presently he reached down and caught her arm, placing it authoritatively in his, and thus hurried her out of the woods. They could barely hear each other speak.

"Don't be so frightened," he cried, disturbed at her pallor, as he almost dragged her along. "I think there is still time enough for us to reach the car, if fortunately one should appear. Ah— don't tremble so!"

Once out of the forest, her strength seemed to return. She broke away from him and ran swiftly down the road. The dusty pike was dimpled here and there with great moist splashes. He was up with her again in a moment, and this time her arm was placed more firmly in his.

"You will make yourself ill," cried St. John, remorsefully; "I have been to blame. If only we can reach some place

of shelter! I shall never forgive myself
if I let you get wet!"

"That seems—oh, it seems such a little
thing," answered Florida, wearily and in-
coherently. Then she added hurriedly,
"I—I am aways frightened in a storm; I
like it, though."

She lifted her head, and a wan little
smile broke over her face. They walked
for some moments in silence. All at
once she paused and looked intently down
the road.

"The car! the car!" she cried.

"Yes, it is the car," he answered. "I
am so glad; I should never have forgiven
myself if I had let you get wet."

His glance sank deep, deeper into hers.

Suddenly with a low, bitter little laugh
she turned away.

The car had stopped, and she sprang
into it, avoiding his aid.

X

When Mrs. Pemberton Jerome decided to make her home in the charming little capital of the Bluegrass Region with the ambitious intention of becoming a social magnate, she ignorantly overlooked in her calculations certain difficulties which did not fail to confront her from the very outset of her career. To her surprise and discomfiture, she did not receive the cordial welcome she had anticipated, the hospitality for which the locality has long been famed being conspicuously wanting.

In spite of a considerable amount of travel and experience in later years, the pretty young widow, whose early youth had been spent in an obscure Western town, had yet to know many things. Among these was the very obvious truth that he who would run with safety must first learn to walk. It had been Mrs. Jerome's great blunder in the beginning that she had startled the inhabitants of this quiet and somewhat exclusive little city by a gait rather too rapid to be sustained with impunity, especially by one so recently arrived in their midst.

The old and well-established Lexingtonian is apt to look askance on all newcomers. In the case of Mrs. Pemberton Jerome, the old and well-established Lexingtonian generally refused to look at all. And as it was the unswerving purpose of this audacious but shrewd little personage to obtain for herself a footing neither slippery nor insecure, she prudently proceeded to slacken her pace.

In the first place, her costumes, which had given offense by their gaudiness and exaggerated adherence to the latest fashions, grew more subdued. If formerly, with her plumes and laces and flounces, she had presented an altogether too gay and costly appearance as she swept through the streets of the old town in her showy equipages, she now affected, with a chameleon-like adaptability, the quiet and more elegant attire of the well-bred people she was accustomed to pass, the result being as propitious, so far as her hopes for future recognition were concerned, as it was softening to her pronounced style of beauty.

She was a strikingly pretty woman, of the plump and dimpled order, with skin like a pearl and an abundance of curling auburn hair, which she wore parted above a very low brow. And when she spoke, it was with a soft, infantile little lisp, and when she laughed, which was quite often, there were two lovely indentations in either cheek; and it was odd but true that, in spite of all this, there was yet a look of hardness about the small face, which must have afforded Mrs. Alexander excuse for persistently regarding her as an adventuress long after she had begun to be received.

It was not Mrs. Alexander's intention ever to receive her at any time. The old

aristocracy could not be too wary, she
affirmed. There was one point concerning which she felt more strongly than any
other: the subject of family prestige.
But how was it possible to maintain this,
if the best people opened their doors to
every unknown individual who chanced to
be attracted to the place? And she said
as much to her stepdaughter one June
afternoon when the two were driving out
on one of the lovely country roads and
happened to meet Mrs. Pemberton Jerome.

The latter, faultlessly dressed in a
cream-colored cloth gown, was indolently
reclining in her pretty victoria with an air
of assurance which Mrs. Alexander found
most irritating. Perhaps her resentment
was heightened by the consciousness that
her ancient and highly respectable coach
with Uncle Abram on the box bore the
contrast but sadly with Mrs. Jerome's
liveried coachman and spick and span
turnout. Of course one might take refuge in the thought that it was infinitely

more in accord with Kentucky ways (and therefore the more desirable) to make use of the carriage owned by one's husband almost since the days of the war, and to be driven by an aged colored servant that had been his former slave; but Mrs. Jerome's newness was none the less an affront, and Mrs. Alexander manifested her disapproval by a haughty gaze into space, when the two vehicles passed each other, which was intended to crush, if not to annihilate.

She sat for a moment with lowered brow, and then suddenly brought herself bolt-upright in her seat.

"Florida," she said, sharply, "your views are so very eccentric upon many subjects, it is impossible to conjecture what your conduct is likely to be in any case; but I particularly wish to know what you propose to do in regard to—this young woman. I consider the advent of such a person in our midst as a crisis in our social life."

They were driving through a delightful

stretch of country leading out from one of the broad thoroughfares. Now and then, under the azure sky, one caught glimpses of substantial old homesteads half hidden in the forests about them, the soft, undulating landscape seeming to melt away into mountains or seas of green, according as there appeared in the distance the dim outline of towering trees, or sunny, waving fields of grain. And on all sides there was an exuberance of nature, a luxuriant rioting of vegetable life that gave one a sense of wholesome satisfaction in the thought that here at least perfection was to be found.

Florida reluctantly withdrew her eyes from the plot of pink clover they were at that moment passing. Her face wore a look of surprise. "In regard to—whom?" she inquired vaguely, her thoughts having evidently been far away.

"In regard to this most objectionable person—this Mrs. Pemberton Jerome, as she calls herself, I believe," the elder woman explained, impatiently.

Florida Alexander

"But why should she not call herself that if it happens to be her name?" A playful smile flitted across the girl's face, and her stepmother turned upon her with severity.

"You would not—surely you would not consider the question of calling upon her?" she demanded, her cold, black eyes fired with indignation.

"I have not considered it," replied Florida, indifferently.

In the brief glances she had occasionally given the "objectionable person" as she passed her from time to time in the streets, she had thought her a pretty, underbred, but entirely harmless-looking individual.

"It is disgraceful," Mrs. Alexander resumed, with an arrogant little sniff, "that a dignified old town like this should open its doors to a person of whom absolutely nothing is known, merely because she has bought one of the handsomest homes in the place (I always particularly admired that house opposite the park) and entertains with a lavishness which, from a stranger, is grossly out of taste. A stranger should not entertain at all. It is shocking—*shocking*. Quite a number have called upon her, would you believe it?"

"I can readily believe it," said Florida, with a laugh. Her glance stole away to the blossoms and lovely green things by the roadside. She was thinking a little wearily of how utterly impossible it would be for her now to take up the life in this place ever again. The idle gossip and comment to which she was constantly forced to become an unwilling listener were growing unbearable. "It is not the provincialism," she sometimes said in feverish rebellion to herself; "the place is not really provincial; it is simply stifling." And as her stepmother continued, there came crowding into her mind recollections of the old college days, of the broad purpose that had been before her once, and of the abrupt, melancholy ending to her high thoughts for useful-

ness, just as if there had been a paralysis
of all her powers.

"She has daring—great daring," Mrs.
Alexander resumed, keeping a strong
grasp upon the topic in spite of Florida's
very palpable lack of interest. "And she
has evidently not the smallest desire for
mental improvement. When asked to
join the 'Progressive Woman's Club,' I
am told that she leaned back in her chair
with that audacious little air she well
assumes, and nonchalantly said: 'My
dear, a club is an excellent place for a
disappointed old maid or an unhappy
married woman; I am neither.'"

"Perhaps she is growing careless of
feminine approval," suggested Florida.

Mrs. Alexander nodded. "I hear she
has the devoted attention of Colonel
Rufus Henry and young Robert Vance,"
she remarked. There was that in her
fretful, metallic voice to-day that irresistibly put one in mind of a parrot.

"Perhaps she finds them all-sufficient,"

replied Florida in cheerful dismissal of the subject.

Mrs. Alexander darted a sharp glance toward her stepdaughter's indifferent countenance, and a malicious smile curled her lips.

"No; she does not find them all-sufficient. I am told that recently a new knight has been added to her list—your Mr. St. John," she said.

Without the flicker of an eyelash or the most faintly perceptible change of color, Florida quietly turned and met her stepmother's gaze. Her cool, unconcerned reception of the thrust was an annoying surprise. Mrs. Alexander grew somewhat embarrassed, but she stoutly held to her position.

"I hear that he is with her constantly —constantly," she declared.

"Then plainly he does not share your opinion in regard to the importance of guarding against her entrance into good society. Not being a Lexingtonian himself, he probably feels less responsibility in the matter."

Mrs. Alexander bit her lips.

"Florida," said she, bluntly, at length, "I think I need not point out to a woman with your knowledge of the world the advantages of matrimony to one situated as you are. Before many years have gone by, the little girls will be ready to be presented to society, and with the wide difference in your ages, your attitude will be anything but comfortable. As for this Mr. St. John, I am free to say I never fancied him myself; I thought him ordinary, quite ordinary. But any one can see that he rather admires you, and I think the match would be satisfactory to your father."

A shadowy smile flickered across Florida's face. "I am sorry, very sorry indeed," she said, "to have to tell you that in spite of the advantages of matrimony to one situated as I am, I shall, notwithstanding, never be any man's wife."

Mrs. Alexander wheeled herself ab-

ruptly about in the carriage, and peered
penetratingly into the girl's face.

"What nonsense, what absurd school-
girl's nonsense is this you are talking?"
she demanded, severely.

Florida was silent. Her lightly spoken
words had left a startling echo in her
own heart.

"No doubt you have had some unfortunate love affair——"

A swift crimson dyed the girl's throat
and cheek and brow.

"And for that reason you think you
are done with all such matters forever.
But at your age it is hardly wise to let
this opportunity slip. A designing
woman like this Mrs. Jerome can ac-
complish a great deal. Moreover, the
woman is pretty, decidedly pretty in her
way. My taste is for a more classic style
of beauty, to be sure," carefully turning
her face to the precise position at which
her profile was to be seen at its best;
"but it is just such a little plump sort of
being as she that two-thirds of the men in

the world would prefer; not that any one
could call you homely, my dear, though
your features are far from perfect.''

Florida broke into a low, spontaneous
laugh, and Mrs. Alexander regarded her a
trifle suspiciously.

''A wise woman never underrates her
rival's strength,'' she asserted ominously,
adjusting more comfortably the airy little structure, composed of artificial violets
and lavender ribbon, she was wearing
upon her head. ''And there is such a
thing as holding one's own charm in too
high estimate.''

The carriage had stopped before their
house. Florida sprang gayly out; a rosy
radiance suddenly overspread her face.

''So you are warning me against Mrs.
Pemberton Jerome?'' she said, smiling,
as she leaned carelessly upon the door for
an instant.

''Forewarned is forearmed,'' the other
retorted, dryly, gathering up her lace
cape with an impatient shrug, and pre-
paring to descend from the coach.

XI

If, judging by appearances, Mrs. Alexander had proved herself unable to provoke the remotest dread or even a momentary curiosity on the part of her stepdaughter touching the attractions of Mrs. Pemberton Jerome, it is equally true that the young widow regarded the girl not only as an acquaintance to be desired, but as a rival to be feared. Furthermore, she was beginning to find the situation somewhat irritating, and was disturbed on being constantly forced to confess that, thus far, the Alexanders had failed to acknowledge her presence in their midst.

They had interested her greatly, the more, perhaps, for the reason that they were quite unattainable. It was, therefore, with a secret satisfaction that she grasped an opportunity afforded only a few evenings after that last encounter on the drive.

There was to be a moonlight fête on rather an extensive scale at one of the beautiful country-homes, and Mrs. Jerome had had the rare fortune to receive an invitation to this, along with most of the prominent members of that circle into which, with a perseverance worthy of a nobler cause, she ceaselessly strove to enter.

On account of certain things in harmony with her well-considered scheme of action, Mrs. Jerome looked upon this event as one of more than ordinary purport. She accordingly adorned herself on the all-important evening with especial care, selecting a black tulle gown, spangled with silver, which, falling loosely from her ivory shoulders contrasted strikingly with her fair complexion, and brought out the tints of her auburn hair. The consciousness that her costume was both effective and becoming fully atoned for its inappropriateness and the fact that the gown would probably be sacrificed in the damp night air. Mrs. Jerome proposed to spend a considerable amount of time in the damp night air; but the sacrifice was to be for a most desired end. She arrived early.

Establishing herself in a large blue satin chair in a conspicuous position in the drawing-room where the guests were being received, she was soon surrounded. Her plans, however, on this occasion, were laid for one.

After the significance of the throng about her had been fully perceived, she adroitly proceeded to diminish the ranks. Finally, only two remained: a young man with a bold, smooth-shaved face, and a stout, blonde, military-looking individual of about sixty, with an excessively pompous manner, who was evidently attempting to monopolize the pretty widow, regardless of the presence of her more youthful admirer.

"Colonel Henry," said she at length,

smiling coquettishly up at her elderly
suitor, as she languidly waved her fan of
black ostrich tips to and fro, "since I
heard that you came originally from Virginia, I have so many times wished to
ask if you are at all related to the man
who said, 'Give me liberty, or give me
death.'"

"Yes, madam," replied the Colonel, in
his deep bass voice, with elaborate gal-
lantry, "I believe there *is* a distant rela-
tionship between my family and that of
Patrick Henry," swelling with importance, and thus deigning to own the Vir-
ginian Demosthenes. "But you will allow me to say," with an insinuating ogle,
and another profound bow, "that I cannot
entirely accept the sentiment of my distinguished relative as expressed in the
words you have just quoted; under *one*
condition I should prefer death to liberty."

"When I was last at the White Sul-
phur," continued Mrs. Jerome, "there
was a Mr. Henry who had previously

been there, of whom I heard a great deal. He stayed six weeks, and in that time it was said that he courted six women—very charming young persons, indeed, and each reported to be very wealthy.''

The man's fat, flabby countenance grew suddenly alarmingly ruddy.

''He left just before I came. I was so very sorry; I am not very wealthy, but I might have been the seventh woman,'' sweetly remarked Mrs. Jerome.

''Madam,'' said the irate Colonel, with a low growl, as he turned on his heel, ''it is my opinion that a damn sight of you women think yourselves courted *when you're not!*''

The widow's sparkling eyes followed the wrathful, retreating figure. Then, stifling a yawn, she broke into a short, bubbling laugh as she turned to her companion.

''Mr. Vance,'' she asked, ''is Colonel Henry a friend of yours?''

The young man looked amused. ''With

a limitation, Mrs. Jerome," he replied. "However, we are on quite pleasant enough terms."

Mrs. Jerome's manner became eager, even intense.

"Then please tell him, do tell him, the first opportunity you have, how destructive anger is to the complexion," she implored.

At this moment Mrs. Alexander and Florida entered the room, and Mrs. Jerome turned a slow, insolent, scrutinizing gaze upon them, her eyes finally resting upon the younger woman with a certain inward misgiving.

The girl's high-bred style of beauty seemed to derive a special distinction from the severe simplicity of her white mull gown, which was cut only a little low and shirred about the neck without lace or trimming. Her arms were bare below the elbow. Her polished brown hair was drawn lightly back from the broad, low brow, and piled high on the well-poised head in a picturesque individuality of style. Three or four old-fashioned cinnamon roses were thrust carelessly into her belt.

Mrs. Jerome did not remove her eyes.

"So I behold the paragon of whom I have heard so much!" she exclaimed, at length, in a sarcastic undertone. "That is Miss Alexander, is it not?"

"That is Miss Alexander," young Vance affirmed. His cool, calculating countenance bore a look of admiration, as his glance followed the girl's movement across the room.

The widow sank back into her chair with an air of being bored.

"Do you think her as beautiful as some of the other people here?" she inquired, carelessly.

"I think her most beautiful," replied the young man, rather absently.

"Do you consider her the most beautiful woman in the State?"

"Perhaps."

She laughed a little in a nervous, embarrassed sort of way, and then leaned

alluringly forward, keeping her eyes play-
fully on his face.

"Do you consider her more beautiful
than—well, than myself, for instance, for
want of a better comparison?"

"I should never think of comparing
you with Miss Alexander," he answered,
smiling, as his glance returned to the
plump little creature at his side. He
met her gaze with a certain boldness in
the look.

"That is a doubtful compliment," she
pouted.

"No."

"Would you not? For what reason,
or reasons, may I ask?"

"For the very obvious one that you
are totally unlike her in every respect.
The fact is," speaking quite seriously,
"I don't know exactly whom I could
compare with her, when it comes to that;
there is something so sympathetic and
broad about her a fellow hesitates to put
her on the plane with other people, some-
how."

"You are highly flattering."

The young man caught himself up with a start.

"I mean simply," he began, rather hurriedly, "that she never—that is, that she could not—oh, hang it! what I want to say is that she would hate like the mischief to hurt the feelings of—of a tramp, even, and that——"

"And that she would be incapable of resorting to the means I have just employed of getting rid of a tiresome acquaintance?"

It was apparent that he was undergoing a certain struggle within himself.

"I believe she would be incapable of that," he answered at length, in a firm, quiet voice.

Mrs. Jerome was silent. Presently she looked up, and tapped him lightly on the arm with her fan. The hard look that Mrs. Alexander had commented upon seemed especially in evidence.

"My friend," she said, coldly, "I have found you rather more entertaining than some of the people I have met thus far; but you have yet to learn one great and important truth: and that is, a wise man never seeks to please one woman by an exaggerated compliment bestowed upon another.''

And having delivered this sage remark, she abruptly turned her shoulder upon him, and fixed her eyes upon some one standing within a few yards of her, and making his bow to his hostess. It was St. John.

The cold indifference upon Mrs. Jerome's countenance instantly thawed into an expression animated, glowing, beguiling. Her fan continued to wave in a slow, measured movement; but her dainty black satin slipper tapped the floor in a kind of restless apprehension. St. John was listening with quiet courtesy to the conventional remarks that were being poured into his ear. His usual grave dignity of bearing seemed especially pronounced as seen in the midst of that brilliant, careless assemblage, and his handsome, dark face appeared very earnest and thoughtful.

Mrs. Jerome's gaze grew intenser, more beseeching. St. John turned and met her look. There was a swift fluttering of the fan, then a decided gesture. He spoke a few words to his hostess—a girlish-looking young matron of a rather striking brunette type—and came forward, an amused, half-indulgent, half-questioning look on his face. As he approached, Mrs. Jerome looked up with a charming air of proprietorship, colored slightly, and dropped her eyes. It was her moment of triumph.

"At last!" she cried, in a low but penetrating tone; "I thought you would *never* come!"

Young Vance arose and offered his chair. Then he walked across the room to where several people were standing.

"Do come with me outside, Miss Alexander," he said; "it is stifling in these rooms. Please come!" and he bore her off with a certain characteristic audacity,

Florida Alexander

the little group about her reluctantly
giving way.

At the sound of the name St. John
looked up quickly. A hot flush mounted
to his brow. Until that instant he had
been ignorant of her nearness, having
had the impression that she would not
arrive until later in the evening. The
girl's light garments touched him when
she passed. He tried to make her meet
his eyes. But the proud head did not
once turn toward him; she was talking
gayly with her companion, and apparently in all unconsciousness. The two
disappeared in the moving crowd about
the doorway.

There was an unpleasant ring in the
laugh which sprang to Mrs. Jerome's lips
a moment afterwards.

"Mr. St. John," she said, "you are
supposed to understand all things, more
or less; it is your métier. I wish you
would tell me one thing."

St. John lent himself rather constrain-
edly to the conversation.

"You are modest in your request, Mrs. Jerome," he replied, "in view of the unlimited knowledge with which you are pleased to endow me."

The little widow darted a swift glance into his unresponsive eyes. She was quiet a moment.

"It is in regard to Miss Alexander," she then said, serenely, lifting a sweetly innocent face to his. "I had heard so much of her before I came to this place, and since I have been here her name seems to be on every one's lips. But the opinions I had already formed from what I had heard concerning her, differ so widely from the opinions of the people here, I am somewhat mystified. Tell me," in most becoming hesitation, as if the exquisite refinement of her nature were suffering acutely because of the question she was about to ask, "do you consider her—does she strike you as belonging (to express it mildly) to the flirtatious order of woman? I should so much like to know if you would describe her as flirtatious?"

"I should not apply the term to Miss Alexander," St. John answered, briefly, and in evident dislike of a continuation of the subject.

Mrs. Jerome regarded him pensively for a time.

"No?" she said, dubiously. "I am so glad to hear you say that. I had really thought her very lovely, and yet you can understand how sometimes just a word can create a prejudice. A woman's reputation is *such* a delicate matter always. Above all things I detest a flirt. How *any* woman can degrade herself to such a low plane, I never *can* understand. And that is why I asked the question; I hoped so much that the things I heard before I came here—one thing in particular—could not be true."

St. John's eyes rested coldly, but without comment upon her. A slow, fierce, terrible wave of anger was rising within him, but he was able to keep an outward control. Stung to the heart by the malicious cruelty of her words, and despising himself that for one instant he should be thus disturbed, he managed to say with quiet positiveness:

"It is impossible that any one could speak evil of her, and speak the truth."

"Really? I am so very glad. I have a friend who was one summer at the seashore where Miss Alexander was making herself somewhat conspicuous by ruthlessly ensnaring all the other girls' lovers, and then coolly disdaining the poor men at last. She seemed simply to revel in her power. One case in particular my friend quite dwelt upon," laughed Mrs. Jerome. "A young man, who had come to the place to see his fiancée, happened to meet Miss Alexander at a cotillion. The usual result followed, but with rather a more exciting finale than generally attended Miss Alexander's conquests. Of course, there may be no truth at all in the story—but according to my friend—"

St. John arose stiffly; his face was stern and white with suppressed emotion.

"Pardon me," he said; "my friendship

for Miss Alexander is such that I must
ask you to excuse me from discussing her
further, especially in such a relation.
There can be no question that you have
confused her in your thoughts with some
other person, totally unlike her.''

Mrs. Jerome flushed scarlet. For the
first time it had clearly dawned upon her
that she had blundered in her eagerness
to make a discovery as well as to strike
a resentful blow. And the discovery had
been complete. The loyalty, the unswerving faith, the high devotion which
shone from the man's set face rebuked
her to silence, while it awoke within her
vague stirrings of reverence for something which she could only dimly comprehend. She had played for high
stakes, and thus far she had lost. But
she was not yet ready to admit that the
game was at an end. With the reckless-
ness of despair, she proceeded to make
the most of the resources at her command.

Quickly recovering from her mortifica-

tion, she assumed an expression of guile-
less unconcern. If it was true that by
that audacious stroke she had only more
tightly riveted the chains that bound
him, perhaps even yet he might be made
to recognize her strength.

"Of course I have made a mistake," she
admitted, adroitly;—"now that I think
of it I believe the name was not Alexander, but something a little like it—Allen-
der—Allison—Anderson—I quite forget;
some other beautiful Kentucky girl no
doubt. There are so many. The fact
is, I paid very little attention to the
story; that kind of gossip does not at all
interest me; *chacun à son goût.*" Mrs.
Jerome had not had sufficient opportunity to know that the adored upper circles
no longer make use in their conversation
of odious little French phrases execrably
pronounced.

She sprang cheerfully to her feet, giving a surprised glance about the room.
Every one had gone outside. She lifted
a helpless, rueful face to his, and then

broke into a low, gleefully exultant laugh.

"You see you can't desert me," she cried, as she quietly slipped her arm in his. "Come! I know the loveliest little moonlit arbor, and we can be quite alone."

XII

It was more than an hour later before he succeeded in making his escape; Mrs. Jerome was not a woman to be easily thwarted in her design, and her design had been as firmly fixed as it was little to be respected. But whatever passed between the two upon that occasion must have been sufficient, so far at least as she herself was concerned in the matter, to carry the weight of a salutary conviction; for she appeared to realize at the last that forever afterward there must remain one man for whom her coquetries could not be displayed.

In every summer there is one perfect day—a day in which Nature, having reached the height of her beneficence, seems to riot in her own excess, and with almost reckless prodigality to exclaim:

Florida Alexander

"Here, I give you all." And to the night that follows such a day belongs especially that melancholy touch of mystery, rapturous, prophetic, which pierces the heart and thrills the senses to such unspeakable things. St. John stood for some moments alone, looking down the dim vistas of the moonlit park. It was an enchanted hour. The leaves of the great elms were throwing tremulous shadows across the sward, and the wind was sighing in the low branches, with now and again a brief, palpitating note of sadness that was yet sweet and insistent as the whisper of a lover.

Here and there under the trees gay groups were seated, the garments of the women gleaming softly lustrous in the silvery light. But the laughter that floated to him from time to time was like the laughter we hear in dreams. Somewhere in the distance a band was playing, and on the platform that had been erected he caught glimpses of figures moving rhythmically to the music; and these,

too, seemed to take on an element of un-
reality. There was an odd surging in his
brain and a ceaseless hammering against
his temples that made it difficult for him
to think.

Faint as was the impression made upon
him by the slanderous words to which he
had been compelled to listen, yet, in a
way totally different from what had been
intended, they had roused in him a storm
of emotion, which only his mighty self-
command had enabled him to conceal.

Perhaps never until that moment did
he fully realize to what extent a man's
destiny may rest in the keeping of a
woman, and know how powerful was the
hold Florida had taken upon his life.

It had not been his desire that there
should be anything hasty or impulsive in
his manner of revealing to her what he
felt; he was not impetuous, and he was
by no means sure that their last meeting
had brought her any nearer to him.
Furthermore, the extreme sensitiveness
of his nature caused him to shrink a little

from disclosing, even to her, that inmost
holy of holies which he himself could not
look upon but with a certain awe and
reverence, until there had come to him
some assurance that what he offered
would not be despised. But since the
moment that those hateful words of def-
amation had rung in his ears, he had
never for one instant hesitated as to the
course he should pursue. He felt that
he must go to her now, this very night, or
else be untrue to himself. The deter-
mination held him in an iron grasp; he
felt it to be the supreme hour of his existence. And gradually there stole over
his spirit the exalted calm of a high purpose, and his countenance became trans-
figured as by some wondrous inward light.

Where would he find her? He stood
for a time uncertain, then walked quickly
down the moon-flecked avenue. But she
was not among the dancers, and she was
not with any of the people he passed.
He searched for her long, in every direction, and in vain. Perhaps she had grown

weary and gone. A sudden thought stabbed him and brought him to a halt. Might she not have become disgusted in witnessing the exaggeration of Mrs. Jerome's too familiar welcome? His nature was distinctly simple and sincere; he knew but little of women, but he felt intuitively that the best of women may sometimes be unjust.

There was but one other place where it was likely she might be. He recalled that in a distant part of the grounds there was a miniature lake overhung by willows —a delightful spot. If only he should find her there!

But on reaching the place, again he was disappointed. The retreat appeared entirely deserted. A delicate mist had begun to rise. The air was heavy with the dank odors of wild grasses and of the marshy soil. Only the hoarse voices of the frogs mingling with the staccato notes of katydid and cricket broke the stillness. He sat down on a rustic bench not far from a tiny bridge which overlooked the water. It was evident that she was not to be found.

He had, however, been here only a short while when there began to steal over him that peculiar sensation which tells one he is not alone—the vague consciousness that suggests the near presence of another human being, invisible yet most vitally real. But when his eyes again searched the obscurity about him, he could find no one. Presently, in restlessly shifting his position, he saw a shaft of moonlight shoot like a star through the thick trees and fall slanting upon a white, motionless figure, half-concealed by the mist, on the far side of the bridge.

He rose quickly. His heart stood still for an instant, and then began to throb painfully; the pose was unmistakable. And even in that moment he was sensible of a thrill of satisfaction in the mere outward perfection, the thorough high-breeding that could give so marked an individuality.

Florida was seated upon the stone steps

of the bridge, her head resting against the slender parapet. Though she appeared to be looking intently in his direction, she did not speak nor stir when St. John started toward her.

He moved a few steps forward, then paused abruptly. In another moment he was to stand before the woman he loved to offer the highest that was in him, the best that was his to bestow; and as the full meaning of it all rushed upon him, along with the joy of this realization was the gravity of the conviction that whatever her answer might be, life for him henceforth could never, never be as it had been.

There was an almost religious reverence in his manner when he approached her; and as he stood looking down upon her, for an instant unable to speak, something seemed to reveal to her the nature of the words that were trembling on his lips. She drew back a little into the shadow, shrinking visibly from what his expression told her. There was the look of a startled deer in her brown eyes.

Florida Alexander

The moonlight fell upon his face, and she saw the spasm of pain that swept across his features at her silent, involuntary protest. But immediately he had seemed to wrap himself in the stern quietude of one whose purpose is unalterably fixed.

She recovered herself with an effort; a smile flickered about her mouth and was gone, leaving the muscles strained and suffering.

"Have you also become 'a companion to owls?'" she asked, in some constraint. She would not meet his eyes, and again her nervous withdrawal from him pierced him like a spear.

He did not try to answer; he had not any words. He only moved a little nearer to her; and then the passion that was in him got the better of his long control.

All at once he reached forth his hands and caught both of her own in his, almost crushing them in his strong grasp.

"Florida! Florida!" he cried, his

whole nature seeming to lend itself to that brief, ungovernable outbreak. But in another moment he went on more calmly:

"You will hear me—you will let me tell you what has been so long in my heart. Ah—you must hear me!"

She had drawn away her hands. They were cold and trembling, and he could hear her heavy sob-like breathing; but there was nothing of resentment, nothing of wounded pride, only a dumb, beseeching agony in her eyes. He was moved to a swift contrition.

"Forgive me," he whispered, huskily. "I was too hasty; I should have given you time. But, oh, you cannot know all the things that have driven me to you to-night. I had sought you everywhere, but I felt intuitively that I should find you here. I knew that there could be no peace, no rest for me until you had looked into my heart and read what is there for you. Believe me I have never spoken to any other being as I wish now to speak to you. I am ready to disclose the inmost recesses of my soul—and there is nothing, nothing that I could desire to keep back from you. My life, my future, my work, my every hope—all, all are yours to do with as you will.''

He paused a moment, and then added in a low voice:

''I have dreamed of such love as this—the love that I should give to that only one whose nature should be as spotless as your nature has revealed itself to me, and whose capacity for loving should be as boundless as I have always felt was yours. And had you been less perfect than I have found you to be, whatever would have been the feeling that I had given you, it could not have been love. It is the passionate purity——''

She put up her hands quickly to her breast, and he halted suddenly. What was the meaning of that strange look she bent upon him?

Her lips were slightly parted, and they were dry and parched as if scorched with flame. Her wide eyes were fixed upon his face with an indescribable expression of compassion and entreaty. She sprang to her feet, and ran a little distance up the bank. But he was at her side at once.

"What would life be to me without you now? Florida—oh, my love—my very life!" His voice broke with dread and longing.

The man's white face near her own betrayed the anguish of his suspense. For one instant her eyes met his.

"God forgive me that I must make you suffer so," she muttered slowly, at last; "I can never forgive myself."

"But why—why need we suffer?—both of us as we do?" he cried in savage rebellion. But his heart was a leaden weight within him, and the words rang out hollow and desolate into the darkness.

She was standing a few feet above him on the rising ground; and as he looked up into her face, the white mist closing about her and seeming to bear her as on a cloud from his sight, there was that in her manner which wholly confirmed the despair that had entered his soul.

His arms fell limply to his sides. He half turned away that she might not see the anguish he knew must be written in his face. He was utterly hopeless—convinced that pity was all that she could ever give him.

"Farewell," she whispered, tremulously, the words seeming to breathe themselves upon him like a sigh from the woeful willows. But he could not speak. He stood with bowed head, waiting for her to go.

About them was the sad mystery of the summer night. From down by the water, like the fateful, recurring note of a bass-viol, came the grave voices of the frogs.

With a smothered sob, she drew a step nearer. As by an uncontrollable impulse, her form seemed to sway for an instant toward him; then she bent quickly down, and lightly as falls a rose-leaf to the earth, her lips touched his brow.

When he lifted his head she was gone.

XIII

At the next meeting of the Board of Trustees, which occurred on the following Thursday morning, St. John went before that body and formally tendered his resignation of the professorship he held in the State College at Lexington.

He stated briefly, in explanation, that certain recent alterations in his affairs would necessitate his living elsewhere in the future; and after expressing a cordial appreciation of the uniform generosity he had received from all persons officially connected with the college, asked that he be allowed to offer such aid as was in his power toward the satisfactory filling of the chair left vacant by his somewhat unseasonable abdication.

His conscientious manner of discharging the duties he had assumed, his high scholarship and inspiring influence over his pupils had caused his services to be regarded as especially valuable. It was with evidences of genuine regret that his resignation was finally accepted. But something in the quiet dignity of the young man compelled the belief that his action in the matter was unavoidable, and in the few farewell words he forced himself to speak there was the throbbing note of a sorrow so deep and private as to render all further flattering suggestion of a reconsideration of the step wholly out of taste.

He experienced a grateful sense of relief when he was at last permitted to withdraw. The outward calm he had manifested from the first was beginning to give way a little under the warmth of the courteous Southern kindness he had just received. Profoundly touched, he stood for some moments in one of the wide doorways looking down, with saddened eyes, upon the broad campus, and seeming to see his own lonely future stretching out before him in the far-distant horizon. Then he walked slowly down the long flight of steps, pausing again, when he had gone only a few yards from the building. Never had the extensive grounds surrounding the college appeared more beautiful.

Beneath his feet was the rich velvet of the incomparable bluegrass; overhead the glowing sapphire of the Kentucky skies. The perfume of many flowers was in the air. There was an almost blinding splendor in the fall of the happy sunlight. And yet, from on every hand —vague antepast of death—came that faint, persistent hint of decline which sometimes makes itself felt even in midsummer. To St. John the suggestion was prophetic. He could only believe that for him the summer of life was ended, and that the autumn had now prematurely begun.

His eyes wandered away toward the edge of the town and to the plenteous fields and timbered country that lay beyond. He had grown strongly attached to the view. Often on clear winter afternoons, having been detained until nearly sunset at the college, he had stood looking wistfully out upon that picturesque landscape with blended emotions of loneliness and delight. And in those moments there was often in his heart something of the same warm and tender devotion that the inhabitants of this region give to their soil; for he had soon ceased to think of himself as a sojourner merely.

Here, in healthful, pleasant work—every year bringing to him a broader development of his powers, the securer acquisition of friends—he had hoped to spend much of his life. But in the deep melancholy that possessed him now through the contemplation of his broken dreams and interrupted plans there was no bitterness, no reproach.

Knowing that it was for the last time, presently he turned and walked briskly to the gate; and the silken rustle of the maples was like a sigh of farewell in his ears. But there was only a look of quiet renunciation upon his features, when he set his face steadfastly toward the town.

There were a number of people whom he wished to see before leaving, and he proceeded to seek these at once. All the morning the necessity of calling at the Alexanders' had weighed heavily upon him. But on reaching the house he found no one at home. When he heard the final click of the iron gate behind him, he brought his teeth tightly together for an instant; then, without another backward glance, he went rapidly up the street.

He spent the next two or three hours carefully packing his books in order that they might be sent to him without damage later on. His lease upon the cottage would not expire for several months, and he decided to leave his belongings where they were, until his plans had become more definite. For the present, he was possessed of but one wish, and that was to get away as soon as possible,

though he well knew that he could not
thus escape the fierce pain with which he
had wrestled through all the dark hours
of the previous three days and nights.
That he would surely carry with him, for
he fully realized that with him it could
only end with life; but if he must suffer
he was resolved that he would not suffer
weakly. In the resistance he was making there was something more than a
man's instinctive combativeness. A certain sternness was stamped upon his features as he bent above his books. Never
once had it occurred to him to abandon
the fight. Life for him had been made
up of disappointments, small and great,
and the last and greatest of disappointments must only be endured with the
same calmness with which he had shown
himself capable of meeting all misfortune.
But by means of solitude and study and
persistent struggle he was determined to
do what he could toward regaining the
tranquillity of spirit he had lost; and by
thus retiring into himself he felt assured

Florida Alexander

that peace would come to him—some kind of peace at least. And though he had thought much and knew many things he had yet to learn that love is real, unsatisfied though it may be, implies a blessing by its mere existence, and that not to any man did peace ever come through a stoical endurance of fate.

For a few days after St. John's departure his name was on everybody's lips, and then a lethargic indifference to all matters not of an immediate personal concern settled upon the old town with the coming of the intensely warm weather, and apparently he was forgotten.

Mrs. Alexander, hearing that he had left abruptly and with but little apology, put her own construction upon the proceeding. While still steadfastly insisting that for her own part she could see but little in the young man to admire, she manifested her displeasure in his sudden exit by such a cold disapproval of her stepdaughter as would have rendered that young woman most uncomfortable, had Florida not been sustained through the ordeal by a certain humorous appreciation which often forced the amusing side of a situation upon her in the midst of actual suffering. Furthermore, there occurred a slight cessation of hostilities, through the distractions of a preparation; for Mrs. Alexander had decided that she would take the little girls and go for a month's visit to the seashore.

"It is such an excellent opportunity, now that you are here to look after your father," she declared, on the morning of her journey, to Florida, who was assisting in the packing of sundry delicately fine garments, which Mrs. Alexander was unwilling to entrust to a servant. "The children look as if they needed a change, and the place has grown insupportably dull. Not a ripple of excitement since the strange departure of that *unsatisfactory young man*," as she now designated St. John, "until last night's announcement of the engagement of that odious Mrs. Jerome to old Colonel Rufus

Florida Alexander

Henry. It is impossible to understand what attraction he finds in the little creature with her turned-up nose and freckled face."

Mrs. Alexander drew a step nearer to the mirror, and surveyed her full-length reflection with complacency. She thought the bows of light blue velvet ribbon upon her white silk morning-gown a trifle too far apart. She turned her dark head with its elaborate arrangement of coils and curls slightly to one side. "The fact is," she concluded nonchalantly, "as you may have heard me remark before, I only care for a classic style of beauty."

"It is much to be preferred," assented Florida, not looking up from the crimson brocade she was carefully folding.

"It is true the woman is rather—rather plump, perhaps. I grant her that. Thinness is fatal. You really ought to take a tonic, my dear," said Mrs. Alexander.

"Thank you for the suggestion; but I don't think I need a tonic," replied Florida, quite amiably.

Florida Alexander

"But you are distressingly thin; but for that pink gown you have on you would be ashen, positively ashen," insisted Mrs. Alexander. "And you have lost much of your vivacity. They say that Wampole's cod liver oil is an excellent cure for the kind of morbidness that seems to be wearing upon you. Really, if you had been taking Wampole's cod liver oil for the past three months, I am quite sure that that young man would never have been able to tear himself away. However, it is just possible that he may return."

Florida dropped the waist of the crimson brocade with a comical smile of surrender. At first her shoulders heaved convulsively, as if she were struggling to enchain the merriment that was bubbling up within her, then her laughter broke loose, and peal upon peal echoed through the room in such a quick transition from sadness to mirth that Mrs. Alexander stood amazed.

"It is your French blood, I suppose,

my dear,'' the elder woman remarked dryly, with a shrug of her ample shoulders, as soon as she had recovered from her surprise. "But if I may venture to advise, I think it would be well for you to cultivate a greater evenness of manner in the future. Such a hilarious manifestation as you have just indulged in could never be regarded as good form. I must ask your father to keep you reminded during my absence of certain little faults to which you seem especially prone, and which every one should guard against."

But the Major had no intention of exercising his authority toward the development of an improved decorum on the part of his daughter. He was entirely satisfied that her breeding was perfect in every particular. But having taken firm grasp upon the idea that her failure to read good books was the whole cause of whatever mental uneasiness he discovered in the girl, for a considerable time he had set himself to work to bring about a reformation in the direction of a higher literary standard.

Accordingly, he continued to spend hours with her every day, reading aloud from his favorite authors, and calling her especial attention to such passages as he wished to take root in her thoughts. She had proved herself to be an excellent Greek and Latin scholar, even from his exacting standpoint, and he was often astounded by her cleverness of insight as well as her picturesque rendering of the text.

These morning hours of study were somewhat lengthened now that the old house was so unusually quiet; and Florida seemed to yield with ready acquiescence to his plans, her trained powers of concentration thus affording her a brief respite from much that she was trying to forget. But the afternoons she always gave to Tim. Nothing was ever allowed to interfere with the time she had appointed for the little fellow's instruction and amusement. And perhaps to no one else did she so unguardedly reveal herself in the long summer days that followed.

The wild gayety that so often possessed her now seemed to cause the boy a painful perplexity at times. His expression would grow grave and wondering, and he would suddenly pause and look searchingly into her face, startled, mystified, and sorely troubled by something in her manner he was unable to comprehend. The strange brilliancy of her aspect, her laughing speech, which had in it a note of wildness, seemed to give him an odd, creeping sensation that was almost akin to fear.

One rainy afternoon she had been entertaining him by explaining the game of battledoor and shuttlecock in the long hall.

He could scarcely attempt to play, fascinated as he was by the lightness and dexterity of her movements. Now and again, she broke into a spirited jest, chiding him for his awkwardness, and a gleam like the scintillation of a jewel shone in her dark eyes. All at once, as she darted past him, her lithe form bending in sinuous curves, her red lips parted and smiling, Tim caught her timidly by the skirts.

"Be you a witch?" he cried, in a bewildered, frightened tone. "I hearn tell o' them."

Florida paused instantly, and her face changed. She stood looking down upon him for a moment in silence, and then slowly, sorrowfully, as if the words were being wrung from her against her will by the child's demanding gaze, she said softly:

"No, Tim, I am not a witch; I am only the most miserable woman in all this sad, sad world!"

XIV

Summer had given way so noiselessly to autumn, Florida scarcely realized the variation, preoccupied as she had been, until she suddenly awoke to find the Kentucky woodlands touched with a royal splendor and the sumac and golden-rod abloom on the roadsides.

She had been spending a week at the country-place of a friend, and one serene afternoon she was driving home alone in the lumbering family-coach which had been sent out for her, when, for the first time in months the beauty of the earth seemed to make its old appeal. For the moment, all the lost glory had returned with the lovely light of the mild autumnal haze.

Uncle Abram shook his head in rueful recollection of his unfinished labors at her repeated insistence that he should slacken his speed in order that she might enjoy the drive to the utmost. The cool breeze wafted pungent odors of walnuts and wild-grapes through the open carriage windows. Picturesque hay-ricks dotted the landscape, and here and there in the mellow sunshine laborers were cutting the dry corn-stalks and stacking them into conical heaps in the peaceful fields, the voices of the men ringing out blithe and clear upon the frosty air. Sometimes a tuneful negro melody, with its pathetic minor strain—sad hint of a former thraldom dumbly endured—fell upon the ear. And now and then the eye was caught by the blue smoke of a distant dwelling, and there came the thought of cheerful hearthstones and of those dear human ties which mean the best of our existence here.

Florida's face was rosy under her broad, black-plumed hat, and there was a healthful sparkle in her eyes wholly unlike the fitful gleam which had sometimes startled little Tim.

All day there had been over her an

unusual sense of anticipation, and she was conscious of an exhilaration of spirits she was at a loss to account for. But often, during the weeks of tremendous agitation that followed, her mind traveled back to that drive in the benign autumn sunlight, and she thought that she understood.

On reaching the gate of her home, her buoyancy was suddenly altered to a sharp foreboding. The children, who had been flattening their noses against the nursery window in evident impatience for her arrival, ran frantically down the stairs the instant they caught sight of the carriage, and now came hurrying toward her out upon the lawn, their little dark faces serious with the importance of a grave communication.

If some evil had befallen her father—if he should be ill! Florida's heart sank with apprehension. She descended quickly from the carriage, and then stood waiting for the children to approach, unable to move another step.

Florida Alexander

"I bid to tell her, I bid to tell her," shouted the little girls, simultaneously, as they ran.

"Oh, Florida, the most awfulest thing has happened!" cried Louise, the first to break the news. She rested her meager form against the iron gate, and paused for breath, her shrewd, gipsy-like countenance betraying a secret satisfaction in the excitement of the moment.

"I said *I* was going to tell her," whimpered Ethel, struggling to push her sister aside. "I bid first, you know I did, Louise, while we were coming down the stairs."

"Shut your mouth, missy; I don't care whether you did or not, I'm going to tell her myself," retorted Louise, defiantly.

Florida caught the elder girl's hands in her own, and held them firmly. "Now, what is it?" she demanded very quietly. She was putting a great control upon herself. "What have you to tell me, Louise? Papa——" but she could go no further.

Florida Alexander

"Papa?" echoed Louise, vaguely, examining critically a slit which she had just discovered in the sleeve of her dark blue flannel gown. "Oh, papa's all right. Did you think it was papa?" raising her head with a look of amused surprise. "Papa never goes hunting. Of course, it could not be papa. It is Mr. St. John."

"Florida, he came back last week to that funny little house he used to live in," here put in Ethel, "and one morning he went out hunting with some men, and his gun went off, or somebody else's gun went off, and I don't know whether mama said it was Mr. St. John's gun or somebody else's gun—whose gun was it, Louise?"

"Oh, go on, if you know so much about it; just go on," replied Louise, with lofty disdain.

"Louise, you know I heard mama," burst forth the other, reproachfully, goaded to tears. "Mama was in the blue parlor with some ladies, and I heard her, every word. I was hi—hiding behind the so—sofa, and I heard her tell—telling everything.''

''Yes, and I'm going to tell her on you, too, you little cry-baby, you. What did she say she'd do to you, if ever she caught you at that trick again?''

''Oh, but you were there, too!'' shrieked the child, in a frenzy of alarm. ''I saw you be—be—behind the curtain —all the time.''

Florida stood mute and motionless. Her face had grown very white.

''Are you telling me that Mr. St. John has been hurt?'' she asked, at length. But there was something strange in the sound of her voice, and the two children instantly stopped their wrangling, and looked up, startled, into her face.

''Oh, Florida!'' they both cried together, drawing back from her in dismay. Evidently the pleasure they had anticipated in imparting a tragic piece of information had been somewhat overrated.

''You look just like *you* were going to die, too,'' gasped Louise.

"No—no—I am not ill," answered Florida, quickly. "Tell me—tell me at once everything you know." And then Louise began again, but this time with less animation.

"He was out hunting, and there was an accident, and they brought him home, and last night he was a heap worser than ever, and when the doctors left him they said he couldn't live, and that he was 'most dying then, and I think he's dead now, and——oh, yonder comes the calf. How could it have gotten out! Let's chase it, Ethel!" And off they flew, their long hair fluttering like pennants in the wind.

After they were gone, Florida remained standing for a moment where they had left her, staring blankly in the direction of their retreating figures. Then she pressed her hands to her temples in a puzzled way and leaned heavily against the iron fence. Their voices were still ringing in her ears, but at every instant the words seemed to grow louder and

louder until they had become at last only
a deafening, unmeaning roar. She was
wholly unable to act or think. There
was a strange glimmer over the earth.
The pavement seemed trying to leap to
her. Her eyes were wide and staring,
and there was a slight twitching of the
muscles about the mouth; but her features were set—almost hard in their pallor. Presently she began to creep slowly,
aimlessly, along the side of the fence, still
clinging to the railing.

But all at once, like a white shaft of
light forcing an opening in a black cloud,
into the darkness of her brain there
pierced an animating thought: *she would
go to him!* And instantly her whole being bounded to the single impulse. Con-
ventions of society, circumstances of the
situation, what were they to her now?

St. John's old colored servant met her
at the door. The woman's face was
swollen from weeping, and there was a
tragic significance in the grave dignity
with which she raised her tall form to its

full height and stood towering above the quivering, breathless, beautiful young creature on the steps below.

Florida winced a little under the reproach she thought she saw in the woman's glance. With lowered lids she waited an instant, white and speechless, a great humility upon her; then she mutely lifted her eyes, beseeching, eloquent in the pathos of a dumb appeal. The expression of the old negress changed.

"He was outer his haid this mawnin'," she hinted, with a world of meaning in the tones. Not receiving a reply, she drew a step nearer, in order that she might whisper into the girl's ear something that was meant for one alone.

"Honey," she said, softly, "he's been axin' fur you all th' time; I 'lowed I gwine fetch you, ef you didn't come 'long soon."

The two women looked each other in the eyes, being drawn oddly near together in that moment of mutual woe.

It was a gaze of entire comprehension with both.

With a beckoning nod over her shoulder, and muttering to herself in the low, crooning voice that had lulled many a babe to its slumbers, old Phyllis placed her hand upon a door which opened into the hall. Then she noiselessly turned the knob, at the same time giving the girl a gentle little push forward. "He's 'sleep," she whispered; "I'll be 'long bime-by."

Florida moved a few steps into the room, paused and put up her hands quickly to her breast. A stifled moan broke from her lips, leaving her as one petrified where she stood. A parting ray of sunlight was stealing in at the window, resting upon the coverlet and upon St. John's white, upturned face. That one look had told her that it was death. She could not let her eyes rest upon him again. But there was something majestic in the deep tranquillity of his repose, and in the expression of those still features she found only a message of peace.

Blinded by remorse and grief, all the suppressed tenderness of her nature touched by the thought of his suffering— especially the suffering that had come to him through the concealment that conscience had compelled her to practice— with a groan she staggered forward. Even in that moment she was conscious of a sense of almost triumph in the realization that at last, for this one time, she could tell him what he was to her. Death had given a right which life had denied. The next instant she was on her knees at the bedside, and her arms were about his neck and her tears were wetting his cheek.

But suddenly she uttered a startled cry and drew back; she had made a mistake. For it was not to lifeless ears, as she supposed, that thus her long-guarded secret was told.

XV

The turn for the better in St. John's condition, coming at a time when his life had been almost despaired of by his physicians, was variously accounted for on the part of those learned functionaries, each of whom believed that the credit of the possible recovery should be traced to his own skillful suggestions in regard to the management of the case. Be that as it may, it is true that waking in the afterglow of a certain October sunset, St. John had opened his eyes upon a world which seemed to reveal to him less of earth than of heaven; and from that hour his fight for life began with a resolution that had been lacking at the first. But it was a hard fight, and more than once it appeared that death would be the victor.

Florida Alexander

During those weeks of suspense, Florida had seemed possessed of a strange new dignity—a kind of secret exaltation that lent a grave sweetness and reserve to her demeanor. It was as if she had come into a deeper comprehension of a great mystery, and walked always under the rays of a divine effulgence, and with a halo about her head.

There is little space for calm, clear thinking when a sudden wind of destiny has lifted one to the heights; and the eye of the beholder is apt to be dazed from gazing too long at the sun. Though she would sit alone by the hour, wrapped in a deep quietude, her hands folded on her knees, her thoughts were not toiling with the problems which the future would surely bring in the case of St. John's restoration to health; all her former questionings were stilled — drowned in a golden sea of rapture, of reciprocated joy. Thus, for a time, the old warfare between that stern, acquired sense, which calmly sees and condemns and that entirely human instinct which is blind and only feels, had ceased. For, though the chances were in his favor, for many days St. John's recovery was not assured, and to-morrow—who can think of to-morrow weighted with the stress of to-day?

But at last the long waiting seemed at an end, and there came a day when the message that went forth was no longer cautious, but positive and final: he would get well. To Florida the news first came through Aunt Phyllis.

With admirable tact, and the practice of sundry roundabout methods, including frequent visits to the Alexander mansion upon errands readily improvised, the old negress had managed all along to keep the girl informed in regard to the patient's condition. And it was an odd coincidence that Miss Alexander seldom passed the tiny cottage on one of those long walks, which she now daily indulged in, that she did not find this faithful servitor leaning upon the front gate, serenely committing the very offense which she had once so heartily condemned to St. John as one of the vices to be discovered among the younger generation of her race.

Finding her here as usual, as she was returning home in the dusk of a murky November afternoon, Florida paused an instant on reaching the house. A light mist was beginning to fall, and the girl was suddenly reminded to raise her umbrella.

"Will you give him this, Aunt Phyllis?" she said, taking a rose from the buttonhole of her ulster, and tipping the umbrella a little forward to hide the sudden rush of color in her cheeks.

A swift sparkle came into the old woman's eyes, and her teeth flashed in a wide, comprehending smile. She placed both hands upon her broad hips, with an air of playful good-humor.

"He gwine git well," she announced, at length, smiling still, and nodding her head oracularly to and fro. "Honey, he gwine git *well!*"

But all at once she drew herself up with the stately dignity of an offended queen. "You heah what that doctor say this mawnin' 'bout movin' him up yonder tuh th' *horspittle?*" she demanded, sternly, her black eyes wrathful and defiant at the mere mention of her archenemy, as she now regarded the physician in constant attendance upon St. John. Whatever opinions others might hold in the matter, she at least was convinced that the young man's convalescence was entirely due to her own ministrations. "Talkin' 'bout movin' him up tuh St. Joseph's horspittle!" she repeated, with infinite scorn. "Ain't I hed eighteen head o' chillun, an' he come 'long hur tellin' me I don't know mo' 'bout nussin' than them ole maids up thar that ain't hed nary one tuh they name!"

Florida looked up quickly, amused for an instant into a complete forgetfulness of everything save the magnitude of this last statement. Amazed that by any one woman the ancient Hebraic injunction could have been so faithfully fulfilled, she asked feebly:

"Were there really eighteen, Aunt Phyllis?" opening her eyes very wide.

The countenance of the old negress expressed a slight dejection.

"Honey, I tell you," she replied, in some confusion. "I 'lowed th' was nineteen, but they counted 'em up on me an' say 'twa'n't but eighteen."

Miss Alexander appeared suddenly to be deeply interested in the passing of an express-wagon, which at that moment turned the corner of the street.

"Perhaps the doctors thought the loss of sleep and the steady nursing too much for you, at your age," she said, very gently, after a time. "How have you stood the long strain?"

"Some days I feels right smart, an' some days poo'ly; fell down las' week an' jarred my intrils an' got a mis'ry in my side. But I gwine hole out!" defiantly. "Ain't I putty nigh got him on his feet? He'll be 'long down yo' way in 'bout a week.''

In a week! The words were like a sword-thrust in the acuteness of their meaning, and the old woman was not a little bewildered by the white, terror-stricken face that was quickly lifted to hers.

''In a week?'' whispered the girl, in an odd, tense voice. ''Is it possible that —that he may be out in a week?'' She was shivering a little, and she drew the cape of her ulster closer about her. Then she turned abruptly. ''You had better go in, Aunt Phyllis,'' she said; ''this dampness won't help you to keep well,'' and in an instant the slender gray figure was lost in the mist.

Lights were burning in her pretty bed-room when she entered it, and the place offered a cheering contrast to the gloom without. Florida stood for some moments on the hearth-rug, gazing absently into the leaping flames. The expression in her eyes had altered, and her momentary agitation had given way to a preternatural calm. Mechanically she drew off her gloves; and presently, in the same quiet, preoccupied fashion, she began slowly to remove her hat and ulster.

As she moved about the room, her eye was accidentally caught by a letter, half-hidden among the writing materials on her desk, which had been that morning received. The envelope was addressed in pencil, and contained one of those brief but thrilling messages that St. John had occasionally managed to send her during his illness.

In a kind of fascinated stare she stood looking toward it, longing, yet not daring to take it again into her hands. A piteous trembling had seized her limbs; she sank into one of the chairs before the fire. Suddenly she leaned forward and bowed her head upon her knees and covered her face with her hands.

About an hour afterward there was a knock at the door, and a servant announced dinner. Without looking up, she briefly directed him to say that she was tired and would not be down. And thus, slowly, monotonously, like the steady dripping of a single drop of water, the heavy moments wore into the night.

She had gone far back into the past, and with that clearer retrospection that sometimes comes, her whole previous existence seemed to unfold itself in a panorama before her. Twelve! One! Then, ponderously, a clock in a neighboring steeple sounded the hour of two. There had been an intense quietude for a long time; then the echo of the footsteps of some passer-by in the deserted streets came nearer and nearer. She found herself listening vaguely to the sound, roused into a momentary consciousness of things about her by that deep sense of a common humanity which was essentially hers and which always seemed to link her sympathetically to all mankind. With what rueful recollection, what anguish of contrition might not this heart, too, be stirred? The man pursued his lonely way, and again the street was still.

She passed on to the time of her acquaintance with St. John. The fire had burned low, and the room had grown gradually chill, yet all at once the very breath of summer encompassed her.

Beginning with their first meeting, her thoughts rapidly followed the shifting scenes; but before one picture she lingered long.

Her heart was beating wildly. Again the spell of moonlight was upon her; the wailing sweetness of distant music was in her ears and the whisperings of the night wind in the willows blending with the grave voices of the frogs. She even seemed to smell the dank grasses, the perfume of the roses and honeysuckle and elder as there came back to her these low, earnest words:

"Believe me, I have never spoken to any other woman as I wish now to speak to you. I have dreamed of such love as this—the love I should give to that only one whose nature should be as spotless as your nature has revealed itself to me, and

whose capacity for loving should be as
boundless as I have always felt was yours.
And had you been less perfect than I
have found you to be, whatever would
have been the feeling I had given you, it
could not have been love.''

With a heavy sob, she half rose to her
feet. What was that thought that now
thrust itself upon her? What terrible
temptation was she about to meet? As
if shrinking from some evil presence, she
crouched down into her chair, quivering
in every nerve.

''Why tell him—why tell him anything?'' a voice seemed to say. ''How
could you ever make him understand?
Have you the right to deal less mercifully
with yourself than you would deal with
another being, human, like yourself?
And if you should try, would it be possible for you to present the case in such
a manner that he would see things as they
really were? Surely, it is for yourself,
you, just as you are to-day that he cares;
what matters it that your truer nature

has come up out of the ashes of a great humiliation?" And then, lost in the sophistry of a disquieted brain, came the subtlest suggestion of all, "Would it be just or kind to him?"

The first gray streaks of dawn were visible in the eastern sky when a strange resolve took possession of her. Hid away in a secret drawer of an old cabinet and guarded well was the photograph of a man who was dead, but who, living, had loved her beyond his honor and his life. Would those eyes that had so long seemed to accuse her speak forgiveness to her now? Many months had passed since she had dared look upon that pictured face. Her hands shook nervously as she touched the spring and the little jeweled casket flew open. The picture was in her hands.

It was the face of a young man of about eight and twenty, willful, passionate and weak, perhaps, but by no means sensual, and withal most genial and kindly—a boyish, handsome face, possessing a certain winning sweetness and reckless daring of expression.

A mist came into the girl's eyes. She moved softly to the window and drew back the curtain. The sun was just rising, and a glorifying beam fell full upon the picture.

Presently—delicate as had been the dawning of the new day—a faint, flickering hope traced itself upon her sad features for an instant, leaving her countenance pure and exalted under the light of a swift transfiguration. Through her tears she seemed to see St. John's face also, near the pictured one, looking earnestly into hers. She dropped the window-curtain and turned away. A fixed and holy decision was upon her. Suddenly she bowed her head as if in prayer.

She would tell him—tell him everything!

XVI

One mild, gray morning in the latter part of November St. John stood in his open doorway for the first time after his illness.

He was not greatly altered. Already he had begun to take on the look of returning health and vigor, and his dark face betrayed the secret of a deep repose —the restfulness that comes to those who have waited long and suffered much and found their peace at last.

Six months before he had stood in that same spot, looking wistfully but hesitatingly in one direction—the direction of a quaint old homestead with clinging rose-vines and tall white columns which gleamed in the sunlight. Then the house had been almost hidden by the dense foliage, but now it was plainly visible through the denuded trees. On that brilliant May morning when all nature had seemed to palpitate with life and promise, there had been but meager hope in his heart; to-day, looking out upon the unlovely street and watching the hungry little sparrows as they hopped disconsolately among the leafless maples, he felt that for him this truly was the beginning, not the end, and that now he was about to enter upon his spring. Had he had his way, at this moment, the whole earth would suddenly have become beautiful with grass and flowers and musical with the singing of birds and the laughter of soft-flowing waters. Seldom had nature seemed so little in harmony with his mood.

In answer to his request, Florida had written briefly to say that she would see him at eleven. It was now only half-past ten. How the moments dragged!

And it was to be their first meeting. Since that time when he had heard her smothered sobs and felt her tears on his

cheek, and listened to that tenderest of
confessions—which only the noblest of
women can ever make—he had not once
looked into the face which, through pain
or delirium or peaceful dream, had
seemed always near to him. It was only
by a strong effort of will that he was able
to keep back the tumultuous thoughts
that now came surging upon him, threat-
ening to destroy his outward calm. That
he did not wish to lose.

With the cheerful reminiscence with
which one recounts the perils he has
passed, or recalls the scars won in honorable battle, he found himself reverting
to the gloomy day of his return to Kentucky four or five weeks before, when he
had been at considerable pains to persuade himself into the belief that he had
come back solely for the purpose of con-
ferring with the trustees of the college in
regard to the chair he was aiding them
to fill. It had been a poor deception
at best, and this morning he was not
ashamed of what he had regarded as a

weakness then. Presently he took out his watch and studied it fixedly. But there was nothing wrong with the watch.

Only ten minutes out of the thirty had passed.

But as the time drew nearer his exaltation of spirit appeared to sink into a gradual depression—that vague, melancholy which seems to possess certain natures just as the moment of fulfillment is assured. Is it regret for the past, is it dread for the future that brings the momentary shrinking and reluctance? There was a touch of sadness added to the sober resoluteness of his looks when he slowly started down the street.

As he approached the house, a sense of punctiliousness brought the Major before his mind's eye, and he promptly decided that before another day had passed he would betake himself into the presence of that gentleman and humbly suggest that he be adopted into the family in the relation of son-in-law at once.

Florida Alexander

In spite of the kindly solicitude and attention bestowed during his illness, St. John found himself looking forward to this interview with a timorousness that was none the less real because tinctured with a quaintly humorous recognition of his own novel and somewhat trying attitude toward his old friend. The Major's benevolent expression seemed all at once to become changed into something fierce and warlike and forbidding; and in imagination he beheld himself trembling like the veriest craven before an eye like Mars' bent superciliously and threateningly upon him. However, his thoughts were altogether in the present when he finally entered the wide portal and was ushered into Florida's little reception-room to await her coming.

It was a low, square room in the wing with tiny window-panes and a deep window-seat. It was airily furnished in chintz and muslin, and in the selection and blending of color, the subjects of the several etchings on the walls, the titles of the stray volumes here and there, there was a subtle hint of the occupant that was at once delicate and urgent and pervasive.

St. John threw a warm, brief glance about him. There were some red roses —roses that he had sent—in a bowl on the table. His heart was beating fiercely now. The faint ticking of a clock on the mantel seemed to grow louder and more rapid.

Soon there was a light, firm step on the stair. The door of the room had been left ajar, and he could hear every click of her dainty heels as she slowly descended the long flight. Her steps drew nearer, paused an instant, and then came steadily on. He rose and stood waiting.

She had reached the door—her hand was on the panel. His breath came quickly, a sudden light leaped into his eyes.

The two stood face to face.

She moved a short space into the

room, and came to an abrupt standstill, crimsoning deeply, as if some new shyness had surprised her out of herself. She was smiling and her face was radiant, but with a brilliancy that both enthralled and startled. There was a tremulous sweetness in her momentary hesitation.

Presently into her great, glowing eyes there crept a deep and serious questioning. The lids faltered and fell beneath his returning gaze. At each quivering breath the rose at her breast fluttered like a frightened red-bird among the lace and folds of her pale gray gown.

For a moment he could not speak.

Never had she appeared more womanly and sincere; never had that mysterious witchery which she alone of all women had power to shed for him been more complete; and yet never at any time of their acquaintance had she seemed farther beyond his reach. He was at a loss to comprehend whence came the sharp, poignant thrust that pierced him in that instant.

Silent, perplexed, he still stood waiting. A stern impatience was beginning coldly to trace itself upon his features. It seemed as if she would never lift her eyes. But all at once, as if reading his very thoughts, she slowly raised them to his—sad, reproachful, but filled to overflowing with that boundless devotion which some women give and in the presence of which all men feel a certain awe and inward shame.

With a low cry he drew her to him: "At last, at last!" and his arms were about her in a kind of savage tenderness and exultation.

But as his lips touched hers, a burning crimson mounted quite to her brow, and trembling she struggled from his grasp.

She walked over to the window, and drawing back the curtain stood looking out for a long time. He could see, in spite of her strong efforts for self-repression, that she was deeply agitated. But when she finally came back and sat down before the fire in the low chair he placed for her, her manner was sweet and tranquil and unconstrained.

He leaned abruptly toward her, his swarthy face lit with a sudden fire.

"Florida," he said, beseechingly, "won't you *say* it—won't you say it just once?"

She looked up, smiling in gay abandon.

"And what is it you wish me to say?" she asked, evasively.

"You *know*."

"No. *I* have so many things to say."

"Very well; begin. I'm waiting, and I've been waiting a long time. But I don't propose to wait forever."

"I don't know where to begin."

"Begin at the beginning."

She fumbled nervously with the rose on her breast, loosening it from its place and then refastening it in a preoccupied fashion. He watched her in some uneasiness, but still indulgent and willing to humor her, provided she did not carry her caprice too far. He had never before thought her in any degree whimsical, and a vague feeling of disappointment was beginning to creep over him.

"Aren't you even willing to say you are glad to see me?" he asked, in a slightly aggrieved tone, after several moments.

"Yes," she replied. But her voice was so low he caught the one word rather from the motion of her lips than from the actual sound.

"Then you will say it—once—as if you did really mean it?"

She lifted her eyes full to his for a moment, and again their dumb reproach, the complete surrender and unveiling of her inmost nature, thrilled him to the very heart's center. They were both silent for a time. A sort of pitying tenderness throbbed in his voice, and there was a directness and total lack of reserve in his next words.

"I had thought that this moment would never come," he said at length, very quietly. "All those long days and nights that I lay there ill and suffering and exhausted, do you know what was the one maddening feeling that possessed me? The feeling that I had won you only to lose you, and that death was going to separate us at the very moment when we had first begun to live. I did not think it possible I should recover."

She started a little and looked quickly away. A long quivering sigh shook her from head to foot.

"Death never separates — only life," she said.

He looked at her curiously for an instant, and then went on:

"But after the time of danger was passed, and there came calm, painless hours of contemplation, I thought of many things. I dwelt a great deal upon the circumstances that irresistibly led me to come to Kentucky in the beginning at a time when other and more ambitious opportunities seemed within my grasp. I was not without prejudice in regard to the Kentucky people—the Kentucky people of to-day. In the newspapers I had read of the dark tragedies that were continually occurring in their midst; and, in the general way one arrives at conclusions without the aid of experimental knowledge, I had formed an opinion that was as unfavorable as it was unjust. I need not say how unlike what I had pictured to myself in many ways I have found the true situation to be.''

''I am so glad to hear that you love Kentucky,'' she answered, archly. St. John broke into a laugh.

''But it is not of my love of Kentucky that I would like to speak just now,'' he responded, quickly, and you know that very well. Sometimes as I lay there it seemed that my whole previous existence had been merely a waiting and a preparation—for this. I thought of everything —of you, of myself, of our future; and I was glad, with a certain fierce joy and elation, that the temptations and dissipations that appeal to most men had not appealed to me, and that my past life was as clean as it was, so that I might seem a little more worthy of you and of your perfect love.''

She was looking steadily away from him now, and he could see only the tip of one delicate ear, the sweep of the rich hair against the crimson cushion, the rounded curves of her supple form. There was a dreamy note in his voice when he began again.

''I think it must have been before me always,'' he continued, ''the belief that the time would come when I should deeply love one woman — one and one only. Therefore, those fleeting impressions that assail the fancy and those far less worthy emotions that work such havoc in men's lives were not for me. From the depths of my soul I pity all those who in trying to snatch some momentary joy bring a blight upon their natures that nothing can remove.''

She quickly turned her face toward him.

''But are there not some who can only find out poison by tasting every bush?'' And then, in an almost breathless eagerness, she added: "You believe — you believe in regeneration?"

"Perhaps not in the way that you understand it," he replied. He looked thoughtfully into the fire for some moments.

"There is only one subject upon which I think we shall ever seriously differ in our life together," he said, slowly, at length, "and that is the subject of our religious convictions. Concerning these, I hold that every individual should be allowed to exercise his own right: the right to speak of them with all reverence, and the right to refrain from speaking of them at all if he so desires. For my own part, I have never been able to accept the orthodox creeds of Christianity. The divinity of Christ, the vicarious sacrifice, the atonement——"

Something in her expression caused him instinctively to break off. Her eyes seemed riveted upon his face, and he thought he saw a look of sudden horror and revulsion in their depths.

But she did not speak. It did not seem possible for her even to attempt to make him understand the meaning in her own life of that deep, unquestioning faith that had come down to her through generations of believing forefathers, and which, however far she might have appeared at times to depart from it in her practices, had never relaxed its hold upon her.

All at once, by one of those irrelevant flashes of memory which every one sometimes experiences, there came vividly before her a scene from her early childhood. She had been reprimanded for something she had done which she should not have done, and she had grown at once, as was her wont, rueful, and apologetic, and repentant. "Oh, papa," she had explained between her sobs, "the devil spoke to me and he was so near, and God spoke to me and He was so far away, I heard the devil and I couldn't hear God."

She could see the quivering, childish form. Tears came into her eyes and she turned her face away.

She rose and began to move softly about the room in an abstracted fashion, as if almost unconscious of his presence. But she suddenly paused, and stood resting both arms, in an attitude with which he was familiar, upon the back of a chair near to him. Again, with the same torturing presentiment that had assailed him the moment she entered the room, he felt her slow, searching gaze upon him.

There were two burning spots in her cheeks, and her lips were parted. Presently she leaned a little forward and smiled—timid, imploring, absolutely self-forgetful now; and again there were tears on her lashes.

All the poetry in him roused by the womanliness of that appeal, inexpressibly touched, he rose and came precipitately toward her. But she motioned him back.

"No, no—please!" she cried. There was genuine pain in her voice. A cold look crept into his eyes.

"Will you love me in spite of the

thorns and the briars? Will you love me in spite of—everything?" she demanded, when he had resumed his seat. His sensitive ear caught the doubt.

He met her glance a little formally. There was that in her repeated questioning that contained a stab; his egoism had received a wound.

She moved away sorrowfully, and sat down as far from him as the small apartment would allow. He did not see that she was trembling pitifully in every nerve.

"Do you remember that you once told me the tragic story of a friend of yours— the friend whom you loved above every one else on earth?" she asked, abruptly, after a time.

"Yes," he replied moodily; "I remember."

"You said that some woman tempted him to dishonor and then disdained him, and that because of his hopeless love for her and his utter misery that he took his own life; you said that the girl to whom he was engaged to be married, and who

still loved him though he had been faithless to her, died broken-hearted; and you
said that the woman who was responsible
for it all was heartless and cruel and un-
worthy of a thought; you said———"

"Pardon me," he interrupted coldly,
"but the story is sacred to me."

She was shivering as if an ague were
upon her. She sank further back into
her chair, keeping her eyes still on his face.

"I know—I know," she responded in
a low voice. "But tell me, do moments
never come to you when you feel that in
some degree you may have wronged her
—this woman? Do you never think of
her?"

"I do not wish to think of her."

"But may she not have suffered, too?
May she not have gone down into the
very depths of anguish and contrition?
And if she were not deliberately wicked,
only impulsive and swept along by an irresistible force, was it not natural that
she should wish to atone, that she should
send him from her, especially after—if

the realization had come that their love had not been of the highest and best? Oh, when you think of it, the pain and the sorrow of it all—have you no mercy in your heart for her?"

He rose stiffly and stood looking down upon her.

"Why need we make her a topic of conversation between us at this of all moments?" he inquired sternly.

"Because—because I wish to speak of her; I often think of her." And then she added huskily: "I knew—I knew your friend."

He turned a startled face upon her.

"*You — knew — him* — Ballinger!" he cried in dismay, the name breaking reluctantly from him. "But why——" he caught himself up with an effort. His face had grown terribly white. "Then possibly you know this woman also for whom you have twice plead so earnestly?"

"Yes," she faltered. The word was a sob.

"And knowing her, knowing them

both, may I ask why you refrained from
mentioning the fact of your acquaintance
—why you have never told me of this before?''

"I could not tell you before."

"Then why do you tell me now?''

"I must."

Suddenly she covered her face with her
hands.

"I thought—I thought I could spare
you this suffering—I thought you need
never know. I hoped that you would go
away. All the time—don't you remember?—I was trying to make you think I
did not care. I thought I had forfeited
the right to be happy. Oh, *won't* you
understand!'' she broke off wildly.
"Can't you see that the woman you have
condemned and the woman you have
loved are the same miserable one?''

He was still staring blankly down upon
her. His face was rigid and pale as
death. But there was a look far more
appalling than the look of death upon his
features.

Florida Alexander

When, after a long time, she took her hands from her face, an involuntary groan broke from her lips at the sight of the awful devastation she had wrought.

One moment he looked into her eyes, and then turning, he blindly groped his way in silence from the room.

XVII

If the length of an existence, so far as its significance is concerned, should be reckoned by a reference to deeds, not years, it is equally true that we may find an explanation of character development in those profound and terrible emotions which sometimes sweep over the soul, shaking it to its utmost foundations, rather than in the slow processes of evolution whereby we are accustomed to consider its growth. And it is not possible but that the outcome of these experiences should be more or less ethical; that there should inevitably follow a moral advancement, or a moral retrogression, of a stern and enduring order.

The effect upon the two people to whom a test the most critical and decisive

had just been offered was widely dissim-
ilar; to the one it had meant a spiritual
enlightenment, to the other it had meant
a spiritual eclipse. But all that it had
meant to each was something that the
other would never know.

When stricken dumb by the confession
to which he had listened, St. John had
staggered forth from the presence of the
woman whom in flawless supremacy his
imagination had placed upon a pedestal
in his heart, and whom he had worshiped
with all the ideal but self-conscious fervor
of his poetic temperament, it was with
the feeling that Truth, like a fallen
statue, lay broken and crumbling at his
feet.

Three hours later, when he retraced
his steps, the marks of that tragic realization seemed branded upon his countenance.

He found her sitting precisely where
he had left her—pale and motionless, but
with an awful quietude upon her. It is
only the grief that is noiseless which

leaves desolation in its track. He paused involuntarily on the threshold, and entered the room and softly closed the door behind him.

"Florida," he said, in a low voice, standing before her, "I have come back. Surely you *knew* that I would come back?"

She did not lift her eyes.

"Yes," she responded dully, at length; "I knew that you would come back. I have been waiting for you here."

But he did not understand the meaning of the spasm of pain that suddenly shot across her features, nor the flush of utter humiliation that dyed her cheek and neck and brow. That consciousness of a power within herself which, at certain moments of her existence, had thrilled her through and through, had become a scourge to her now.

"I have come to say what you would not let me say before; I have come to ask you to be my wife," he said very quietly.

Her lids were lowered. Her hands lay folded in her lap. Her whole attitude expressed only an unutterable weariness and apathy. She seemed scarcely to heed or even to hear his words. He came nearer and took the chair at her side.

His sensitive face twitched nervously under the powerful struggle he was making for self-control. But his manner was calm and very deliberate. There was something almost hard in the resoluteness of his looks.

"Will you hear me?" he asked gravely, after a time. "Will you try to understand what I feel at this moment?"

Her eyes were resting in a fixed, abstracted gaze upon the smoldering embers on the hearth.

"I will try," she answered simply.

"Then we need not speak of what these last three hours have been." There was a dreamy sadness, a far-off note of self-pity in his voice.

"No; we need not speak of that."

All at once he leaned forward and looked earnestly into her face.

"And you will believe that it is not merely a sense of honor that has brought me back to you?" he demanded anxiously. "In spite of this memory, which we both must bear always, to the very end of our days, do not doubt, never doubt, that I have any deeper desire than that you should become my wife."

"I know," she replied, in the same lifeless, wearied tones; "I know; I have not doubted that." And again the slow, burning crimson mounted to her brow.

He glanced at her uneasily. His teeth were clinched.

"We will help each other to forget," he said quickly.

"No one ever forgets. The very effort to root out a memory only fixes it the more securely in the breast."

He could not answer, and his silence only too surely confirmed his acquiescence. An ominous cloud was settling upon his dark face. He was breathing hurriedly,

and a heavy moisture had gathered on his
brow.

"Death was not strong enough to separate us, nothing can come between us
now," he exclaimed fiercely.

A sharp, quivering note of apprehension resounded through the room.

"There is one thing that should
separate us always." Then in a voice,
firm but almost inaudible: "It is conscience," she said.

And it seemed in that moment that she
had climbed to some great height and
was looking down upon him in the
marshes below.

He started guiltily, and as if he had
been struck. Speechless, he sat staring
at her, with that strange, uncomfortable feeling one experiences when he
knows his inmost thoughts have been
read—the thoughts which, of all others,
he would guard and cover if he could.

Presently she rose and walked over to
the old-fashioned chimney-piece. She
stood with her back toward him for sev-

eral moments. She turned suddenly, and leaned one arm upon the mantel, facing him. She was very pale, but quiet—quiet with that calm which always strikes terror in the heart of the beholder and freezes the blood in his veins.

"Can you not see," she said finally, in low, distinct tones, "that holding the views you do, the very fact of your willingness to turn away from the standard you have set up implies a downward step? Can you not see that marriage between us now would be no marriage at all, that it would be hideous—an unholy thing?"

His face had grown ghastly.

"No," he repied sternly; "not if I wish it—not if we both wish it," he corrected.

She was silent a long time.

"But I do not wish it," she said slowly, at length.

A low, savage cry broke from his lips. There was the flame of thwarted passion in his eyes. He made a swift movement toward her, but she waved him back.

"Whether it be right to love you or wrong to love you, is nothing to me now. I love you," he declared recklessly and vehemently.

Her wide eyes were fixed upon his face.

"Oh! do you think it would be possible for me to live with you as your wife —as your wife," she repeated, in bitter humiliation, "knowing that you did not respect me in your heart?"

He stood silent before her, unable to speak or to move.

"Do you think," she continued, with sorrowful solemnity, "that the time would not come, after the infatuation you now feel had died the usual death, when you would realize the blunder you had made, and despise me for allowing you to make it? But it would surely come; and I — how could I meet that time? And yet," she suddenly broke off, her rich voice rising and vibrating, thrilling him with the old magical sweetness, "as I stand before you to-day, broken-hearted and desolate though I am, trusting no longer in my own strength, feeling even in the anguish of this moment a deeper reverence than ever before for all good and sacred things, I know — I know — that repentance has made me a better woman than the untried being you have dreamed of, than the woman you have thought me to be.''

There was the ring of triumph in the words, the look of a divine victory on her face. And as she spoke, the distance that had been steadily widening between them seemed all at once to become a great yawning gulf which neither could ever cross.

''Will you listen to me for one moment?'' he demanded, curbing the low ground swell of anger within him by a mighty effort.

She bowed her head.

''When I returned to my home this morning I found a telegram awaiting me. It stated that the nearest relative I have in the world, and one to whom I owe more than to any other being, lay ill and probably dying. I shall leave on the first train. Whether I ever return to this place will depend upon the answer you now give me. If you send me away from you now, it will be forever; you should understand this. Once more I ask you to be my wife.''

A look of dumb surprise traced itself upon her features.

He crossed the room quickly, and caught both of her trembling hands in his, almost crushing them in his grasp.

But they were cold. And in that instant something told him intuitively that no fire in his would warm them ever again. His face grew white as marble.

''It was not love, it could never have been love,'' he said, with bitter, merciless conviction.

Her ice-cold hands fell limply from his. He turned abruptly away.

A moment afterward she heard the sound of his footsteps echoing drearily down the long hall, and knew that he had gone forever out of her life.

XVIII

It was five o'clock of the same afternoon.

The great baritone bell in a neighboring steeple had just sounded the hour—sounded it with a serene and majestic indifference to the passing of day—and an instant afterward the fragile little timepiece on the mantel had chimed in delicate accord. The echo lingered sadly in the room, then died away with sweet, haunting reluctance. But Florida heard neither the bell in the steeple nor the clock on the mantel.

There were hurrying vehicles in the streets, the horses' hoofs reverberating noisily upon the brick pavements. People were turning their faces homeward. Children had ceased their play, and were calling farewell to one another across the grassy lawns. Servants were moving through the house. The preparation for dinner was about to begin, and occasionally there was a snatch from some weird negro melody or the quaint jargon of an authoritative command. The room was filled with lurking shadows; the fire on the wide hearth had burned low, the air was damp and chill. But the bowed, motionless figure in the low chair appeared to have lost all power to hear or see or feel.

Presently, like one wakened rudely out of sleep, she started, half rose from her seat, and looked about her with bewildered eyes.

From far down in the town, drawing ever nearer and nearer, came the shrill voices of the newsboys calling the evening papers. Instantly she was roused. Tim! What could have become of the child? Never before had he failed to put in an appearance at the appointed time. A sudden sickening foreboding began to tug at her heart. The boy had been looking pale and thin in spite of all her watchful care; and recently she had been conscious of a growing anxiety lest he might have become a trifle too serious through those long, beautiful talks of theirs.

She glanced uneasily toward the clock. She felt faint and ill. Since morning she had not tasted food, but she managed to drag herself wearily to her room and to get hurriedly into an outdoor costume. In less than five minutes she was on the street.

The cries of the newsboys were coming nearer. But she listened in vain for that rare, pathetic note which was the peculiar charm of Tim's voice—that sweet, remote, indescribable timbre which one so seldom hears in the voices of the children of our land.

Suddenly she paused. An ungainly boy of thirteen or fourteen, as unlike her own "bonnie laddie" as could be, brushed roughly past.

"Here yo' evenin' papers," he shouted

loudly. "All about the accidint! *Leader!*
Argonaut! All about Tim Twine killed
by the 'lectric cars. All about the accidint!"

Florida turned a white, terrified face
upon the boy, reeled a little, and put
forth a detaining hand. "Give me one
of the papers, please," she gasped. Her
teeth were chattering. The boy regarded
her with brutal unconcern as he dived
down in his pocket for the change which
she seemed not to see when he handed
it to her, and which was straightway returned to the place from whence it came.

She took the paper and tried to read.
But her hands shook so at first she could
see only the headlines:

Horrible accident at the junction of Broadway
and High streets! Little Timothy Twine, a newsboy, killed by an electric car while heroically
rescuing a three-year-old Italian child who had
wandered upon the track.

Her eyes ran with frantic but careful
eagerness down the column, an irrational
clinging to hope causing her to scan
closely every sentence; she was still too

stunned to grasp fully the pitiful truth as truth. But presently her glance fell upon these words, and her face blanched to the lips:

As the electric car reached the brow of the hill and started down the steep incline, the motorman noticed a small child running in the street between the car-tracks and directly toward the front of the car. He saw at a glance that unless the child could be stopped death was inevitable. He called to her at the top of his voice, and applied the brakes with all his strength. But the little girl, hearing the cry, stopped between the tracks and crouched down to the bricks, helpless with fright. At this moment, little Timothy Twine, a newsboy known to many of our citizens as a sprightly lad and as the possessor of a marvelous voice, turned the corner of Broadway. Laying aside his bundle of papers, in a flash the boy was in the street. In another instant he was on the car-track and had caught the terrified child in his arms. But just as the car bore relentlessly down upon them, the little fellow's foot slipped on the icy pavement, and he fell. With one last supreme effort, he managed to shove the little girl forward beyond the track, and thus to save her life. The motorman leaned over the front of the car in a desperate effort to catch the boy. He touched but could not grasp him. The grinding wheels went over the body of the noble child, crushing him to death.

Florida Alexander

It was almost night when Florida entered the dreary side street not far from her home. The forlorn abode, which had been Tim's only habitation since his baby eyes had opened upon the world, seemed to have taken on new dignity in consequence of the flimsy piece of white crape which now floated from the doorknob. While yet a long way off, Florida could discern this waving signal of death, and it served as a guide to her in the gathering darkness. At the first sight of it she caught in her breath with a tearless sob, then hurried on.

Now and then, as the slender figure made its way past a grocery-store or beer saloon or miserable dwelling, a curious, comprehending glance was thrown upon her. Her face was startling in its pallor, but her eyes were dry.

There was a crowd about the door, but when she approached, all drew back respectfully. She climbed with a tread that was almost firm up the low, rickety flight of wooden steps, and knocked softly.   The door was opened at once.

Florida moved gropingly into the dimly-lighted room.   Three women were shivering around the fireless grate, talking in subdued tones, and something white and still lay on the bed in the corner.   Even in that moment she felt a throb of thankfulness that the beautiful little face had not been marred.

The woman who opened the door to her, apparently the youngest of the four watchers, stood studying her intently, with eyes that rested in a covetous scrutiny upon the girl's rich furs and well-fitting garments.

"Will you leave me with him alone for a little while?" said Florida in a low voice.   She addressed herself to the woman who had opened the door, but included the others in her glance.   At her request, the three lugubrious women sitting with their backs toward her rose and filed slowly out of the room, but the

fourth remained an instant with her hand
on the knob.

"I will not stay long," the girl added
imploringly, seeing that the woman did
not go. "I—some one may have told
you—I was his friend."

"Lord, miss," replied the woman,
with chattering volubility, "we all knows
how kind you've been, an' what a little
man you made o' Tim. Why, 'tain't
no more'n three days sence he was settin'
on my doo'-steps, an' preachin' a reg'lar
sermon to them boys o' mine—him that
useter be the terror of the whole street
hisself. The big one had been fightin'
the little one, an' Tim he jest laid down
the law 'bout doin' to t'other as you'd
have t'other do to you, an' all the time
he was jest as frolicksome as a young
colt, though them big eyes did grow
mighty soft and shiny when he talked
'bout the things you tole him. I declare,
I didn't know whether to laugh or to cry.
I jest said to myself, ' If Tim ain't a
miricle o' grace'———''

Florida Alexander

All at once she stopped. Something in the tragic face of the girl as it bent above the dead child awed and amazed her. The woman's ready flow of conversation had ceased. Her eyes grew full of wonder and incredulity. "Well, I declare!" she muttered to herself as she softly closed the door and disappeared into the room beyond.

Florida stood looking down upon the little white face that would never again be lifted to hers in the old trustful, adoring fashion—that would never again grow warm and grateful for her smiles, nor roguish at her jests; and as she stood thus, gradually a strange idea began to steal into her benumbed and harassed brain: that she was gazing not upon the lifeless body of the child she had loved and befriended, but upon all the dead hopes of her own existence, which must now be buried forever out of her sight.

The kerosene lamp on the table threw mournful shadows about the bare, white-washed walls of the comfortless room, and

brought into bold relief the two almost
equally quiet figures, which appeared to
take on the emphasis of an emblematic
significance. A hardness had traced
itself upon the features of the girl, whose
eyes were fixed stonily upon the prostrate
form before her. Something seemed to
have dried up all the fountains of emotion
within her. She could not weep; she
could no longer feel.

Presently she drew nearer to the dead
child, and then for the first time a complete realization was borne in upon her of
the manner of his death, of the beauty and
the heroism of the sacrifice he had made.

A long, quivering sigh rose as from the
very depths of her being. She sank
upon her knees; her frozen lips moved,
trembled—and tears, the first that she
had shed in all that agonizing day, gushed
into her eyes.

*   *   *   *   *

Three hours later the Major, dozing
over "The Heart of Mid-Lothian" before

his library fire, looked up startled from his book at the expression he saw upon his daughter's face. The girl had come in very quietly, forgetting to knock, and she had been standing near him for several seconds before he became conscious of her presence. He checked an involuntary exclamation of dismay when their eyes met. But, though the signs of some recent mental conflict were traced upon her features, her manner was now so calm and decided, so tenderly imploring, that the Major was both alarmed and touched. She remained standing a moment, looking silently down upon him with a yearning devotion and pity in her eyes. Then she sat down beside the fire in the small chair in which she used often to sit when a child, and her gaze wandered away to the quaint mantel, and rested thoughtfully upon the blazing logs on the hearth, as if the words with which she would tell him were forming themselves slowly and with difficulty in her mind.

He could never afterward recall what were the arguments she had used, if indeed there had been any arguments at all, whereby she had won from him a reluctant consent; for the strength of her appeal was in its profound spiritual sincerity. She spoke briefly of the call that had sounded for her several years before, and which had never been wholly silenced, to a life among the poor and the helpless and the unenlightened of the earth; of the strong wave of Christian Socialism under the influence of which she had to some extent come; of the plan and purpose of the College Settlements in the great cities; and lastly, of a recent letter from a friend she had met at college who was permanently connected with one of these settlements—a young woman of whom she had made mention to him before, and to whom, with a passionate pleading, she now besought that she be allowed to go. And in the end she had her way.

Only once did her voice falter, and

that was when she touched upon their parting, the pain she must inflict upon him while she went forth in obedience to that summons which again had seemed to come to her with the authority of a divine command.

But when she spoke of the desire that her mission of love and duty should lead her more especially into work among children, tears gathered in her father's eyes.

He rose and laid his hand with a beseeching tenderness upon her head as he bent over her. "I had hoped," he said brokenly, "I had hoped that I might live to see your own children in your arms, my child."

A flush mounted hotly to her brow, and then left her pale and passionless, and beautiful as marble. But the memory of the look he had called into her eyes was something that he would bear with him to the grave.

*   *   *   *   *

Florida Alexander

It was a cool, sunshiny afternoon in the late autumn, with just an invigorating hint of winter in the air. The day of her departure! All the morning she had been busily occupied; but now her trunks were packed, the carriage was at the door, and her father was waiting to go with her to the station. She could hear him moving restlessly about the room below, and, as was his wont when sad or lonely, singing softly to himself—singing one of Dr. Watts' hymns. She sat down helplessly on the side of the couch, and threw a hesitating glance about the little bed-chamber in which she had suffered such unspeakable things. She had fully twenty minutes yet; even now she could alter her decision—it was not too late.

How still the old house was! Her stepmother had bidden her a somewhat impatient adieu, and had hurried off, with characteristic unconcern, to a reception. The children also were away. She had bestowed her gifts upon the servants,

and made a little farewell speech to each.
She had absolutely nothing left to do.
The moments were flying. The voice in
the room below had ceased.

Suddenly two great tears welled into
her eyes and fell with a moist splash upon
her clasped hands.

Everything grew dark and uncertain
before her; an awful blindness seemed
closing in upon her; she stretched forth
her hands with a feeble, frightened cry
—like the bleat of a timid lamb on a
lonely mountain side.

Then, all at once, the great sun burst
from behind a cloud; she felt the strength
of a mighty Arm about her, and in her
ears a Voice was whispering words of
peace.

*   *   *   *   *

When she entered the library she
found him asleep in his chair. His Bible
lay open on the table at his side, and she
knew that, as always in the midst of
every strife, he had been seeking the safe

stronghold of his faith, and that the smile
still resting upon his features was a bene-
diction for her.

And seeing him thus serene and rest-
ful, the afternoon sun shedding a soft radiance in the room and making a glory
about the beloved head, she felt that she
could not rouse him to that awakening of
pain. She stood thoughtful for a moment, trying to decide upon some means
whereby she might leave a message, so
that he should know that she had gone
forth, not in a miserable, cowardly fashion,
but bravely and cheerfully, to her great
life-work—that it was to be with her truly
the victory of vanquishment, and that
there had been given her "the garment
of praise for the spirit of heaviness."

A happy thought came to her. She
moved behind his chair and softly turned
the pages of the Book. Then she drew
a line delicately in pencil beneath the
passage she wished him to read, and
placed a flower upon it. And these are
the words which caught his eyes as he

Florida Alexander

woke nearly an hour later in the sunlit room:

Thou hast turned for me my mourning into dancing; thou hast put off my sackcloth and girded me with gladness; to the end that my glory may sing praise to thee and not be silent.

THE END

IMPORTANT BOOKS
OF RECENT PUBLICATION

FICTION

ON THE RED STAIRCASE. By M. Imlay Taylor. 12mo. $1.25.

> "A strong, bracing story it is, and one which gives us a clear view of an exceptionally interesting epoch in Russian history."—*New York Herald.*

> "The book is exciting, well sustained and excellently written. . . . Another 'Zenda' story."—*Chicago Times-Herald.*

AN IMPERIAL LOVER. By M. Imlay Taylor. 12mo. $1.25.

> "The tale is one of love, of intrigue, and of adventure, and seems to us even better than its predecessor, 'On the Red Staircase.'"—*The Outlook, New York.*

> "A dramatic and intensely interesting semi-historical romance of Peter the Great's court."—*Evening Bulletin, Philadelphia.*

GROUND ARMS! The Story of a Life. A Romance of European War. By Baroness Bertha von Suttner. A new edition. $1.00.

> "The most eloquent appeal for universal peace we have read in years. This story is one of the strongest works of fiction of the present decade."—*The Arena.*

STORIES FROM ITALY. By G. S. Godkin. 12mo. $1.25.

> "A new and most lovable light is thrown upon Italian character by these charming glimpses into life in sunny Italy."—*Herald, Los Angeles.*

A GROUP OF FRENCH CRITICS. By Mary
Fisher. 12mo. $1.25.

> "American readers will be glad to read the able little volume and learn there is yet a saving quality in French literature which they before had not known."—*Inter Ocean, Chicago.*

CHRISTIANITY, THE WORLD-RELIGION.
By John Henry Barrows, D.D. $1.50.

> "Dr. Barrows has given not only to India, but to the thinking people of the world, a book of great merit and value."—*Public Opinion*

NATIONAL EPICS. By Kate Milner Rabb.
12mo. $1.50.

> "The compiler has performed a useful service in making accessible in the compass of a single volume so much material for the study of these noble poems."—*The Review of Reviews.*

JOURNAL OF COUNTESS FRANCOISE KRASINSKA IN THE EIGHTEENTH CENTURY. Translated by Kasimir Dzie-
konska. With portrait and other illustrations. 16mo, gilt top, deckle edges. $1.25.

> "Not for a long time have we seen so entertaining a book as this. It gives, with charming näivieté, a picturesque account of high life in Poland at the middle of the last century—a life still pervaded by feudal traditions and customs."—*Nation, New York.*

EATING AND DRINKING. By Dr. Albert H.
Hoy. 12mo. $1.50.

> "I would exhort all people who want to live long, and be really happy while they do live, to buy or borrow a copy of that priceless book, and study it up as soon as possible."—*Prof. Albert H. Walker, in The Hartford Times.*

THE STORY OF LANGUAGE. By Charles
Woodward Hutson. 12mo. $1.50.

> "It surprises the reader by its wealth of learning, extending in some degree into regions to most students quite unknown."—*The Literary World, Boston.*